I0687729

VOL. 3, NO. 3   **ISSUE #11**

FEATURES

NEW STORIES

CLASSIC REPRINT

FROM THE CAT'S PERCH

A few issues back, I mentioned how proud we were that John M. Floyd's "Rhonda and Clyde," from issue five, was selected for inclusion in *The Best American Mystery Stories 2020* (Mariner Books). Since then, three more of our stories have been singled out for recognition.

John M. Floyd's "Mustang Sally," from issue seven, received a 2021 Shamus Award from the Private Eye Writers of America, and Gordon Linzner's "Show and Zeller," also from issue seven, was nominated for a Shamus. Additionally, my "Blest Be the Tie That Binds," from issue six, was selected for inclusion in *The Best Mystery Stories of the Year 2021* (Mysterious Press) and was named one of the "Other Distinguished Mystery and Suspense" stories of 2020 by the editors of *The Best American Mystery and Suspense 2021* (Mariner Books). If anything, this demonstrates that *Black Cat Mystery Magazine* continues to build on the strong foundation established by publisher John Betancourt and founding editor Carla Coupe.

Which leads to this issue, which contains a dozen stories by writers both familiar and new to us, representing a wide range of crime fiction sub-genres and settings both historical and modern. We hope you'll agree that they're all winners.

—Michael Bracken
Editor, *Black Cat Mystery Magazine*

Staff

PUBLISHER & EXECUTIVE EDITOR
John Gregory Betancourt

EDITOR
Michael Bracken

WILDSIDE PRESS SUBSCRIPTION SERVICES
Karl Würf

PRODUCTION TEAM
Sam Hogan
Karl Würf

DEAD RECKONING
LEONE CIPORIN

Helicopter rotors whipped humid night air across the hospital roof, rustling the document Adam Porter was trying to sign. He tamped down the edge, scribbled his signature, and handed the waiver to the pilot, shaking his head at the absurd ritual. Every time he retrieved a donor heart, he had to promise not to sue Helio if its helicopter crashed and killed him. Adam pictured an army of zombie plaintiffs advancing on Helio's headquarters.

"What's so funny?" The pilot stowed the waiver in his flight book, as his bangs flopped in the rotor-generated wind.

"At three-thirty in the morning, either everything or nothing. Does the donor heart sign a waiver, too?" Adam flashed a grin, prompting a startled look from the pilot.

Adam wiped his expression clean, tucking the nervous energy behind his usual stoic exterior. This trip had to be like any other. He strolled to the roof's edge to settle his mind with a scan of the sleeping city on a midsummer night, watching dribbles of traffic pulse between dark buildings with randomly lit windows.

He approved of cities, and the efficiency of supply and demand settling down together, trading privacy for convenience. Directly below, outside the emergency room, a couple ping-ponged tasks to strap a bandaged, squirming toddler into his car seat. Adam stepped back and kicked a pebble. The world was full of families with maimed children.

"Ready to go," the pilot called out.

Adam trotted across the roof, stopping just short of the helicopter door, blocked by Fritz, the new surgical fellow. He was posed for a selfie, one foot in the helicopter, his shoelaces threatening to tangle in the threshold.

Adam stuck an arm in front of Fritz's phone. "Move. We need that heart." Adam's own heart knocked at his chest, passing along the signal to hurry.

"Just one more, Dr. Porter. Here, stand next to me." Fritz' scrubs puffed in the breeze.

Adam delivered a long, silent stare.

Fritz snapped another picture and scrambled in, grinning as if they were starting an amusement park ride. The grin widened as he opened the paper bag on his seat. "Donuts!"

"They always bring food."

Adam's stomach fluttered. He'd never been nervous on procurement trips before. He nibbled his donut, giving his stomach something to work on.

"Are these regular or jelly?" Fritz asked. "I love jelly donuts."

Adam inspected his bitten donut. "Red velvet cake."

At the sight of the red velvet, the dough in Adam's mouth clumped like clay. He forced it down with a thick swallow and shoved the donut back in the bag, as Fritz stuffed his entire donut into his mouth with the heel of his hand.

The helicopter rose and the city shrunk to snow-globe size. In the circle of urban lights, a utility truck zipped along a boulevard normally clogged with vehicles and students.

"I usually can't go one block in ten minutes." Fritz followed the truck's progress like a kid watching an ant farm.

Adam closed his eyes. He missed Brian, the previous surgical fellow. Brian had been friendly the way people are when partnering with a stranger on a checked-out grocery cart or a repaired vehicle, an arrangement that had worked perfectly, with Brian even joining Adam and Maura for Thanksgiving dinner. Fritz had only been on the job three days, and already Adam couldn't wait for his year to be over.

Adam woke his phone and pulled up a photo of the girl who would receive tonight's heart. Susanna's father had texted him the photo as they stood outside her room, saying, "I want you to think of her smile, Dr. Porter, not just her heart."

Adam enlarged the photo with his fingertips as the copter tilted, a warning that it was about to accelerate. He braced himself against a whoosh that knocked Fritz against his headrest.

"You can see everything!" Fritz bounced back from the whoosh and wiggled against the window, as if the whoosh had never happened.

Adam shook his head. Fritz always ignored things he didn't find interesting. His first day on the job, Fritz had peppered Adam at a patient's bedside with questions about a surgical procedure, not even noticing the patient's sudden pallor.

Adam looked down at the photo. He'd promised Susanna that afternoon: "You'll get a new heart soon. Then you'll feel much better."

Susanna had wrinkled her nose, waving the freckles on its tip. Daisy would've had freckles splattered across her nose too.

"Can't you fix this one?" she said. "I like my heart. I love Mommy and Daddy with it."

Her mother choked off a sob as Adam said, "I don't think we can fix it. But a new heart will love Mommy and Daddy just as much. Maybe more, because it will be stronger." That was what he loved about his job, making the broken whole.

"When do I get my new heart?"

"Soon." Adam turned to Susanna's father. "Children get first priority. The next heart that's a match is hers."

His promise had come true only hours later.

"I bet you've been on a lot of helicopter rides, Dr. Porter." Fritz's grin revealed a bit of donut that had escaped the gulp. "Ever take your family on a helicopter? I promised I'd take Annie for a hot air balloon ride, as a sort of engagement present."

"Isn't a diamond ring an engagement present?"

Fritz chuckled. "Yeah, but calling the ride an engagement gift means the parents will pay for it. Balloon rides aren't cheap." After a pause, he said, "Ever take your family on a hot air balloon?"

Adam's stomach muscles tensed. "No."

"I haven't met your family. I think your wife's name's Maureen? And you haven't met Annie."

Adam stared at passing cloud tendrils. Friendly, ghostly traveling companions. "We'll meet at the hospital's welcome party."

Each July, the hospital welcomed a new batch of residents and surgical fellows, all lacking real-world experience, yet convinced they could handle anything. July was a terrible month to get sick.

"You're around all summer?" Fritz asked. "No travel plans?" His gaze darted around as if a new item of interest would pop up at any moment. His legs flung sideways, taking up more room than needed in the cramped cabin.

Adam pulled his own feet out from under his seat and shoved them in Fritz's direction. He needed to set boundaries early, or the year would be unbearable.

"No travel plans," Adam said. "It's a busy time, with my having to train the new doctors." He arched an eyebrow before glancing out at the growing cloud cover.

"All I want to do with my time off is sleep," Fritz said. "I can't believe how tired I am already. I think I could sleep an entire day and still be tired."

Adam was tired too, but he'd been awake when the three o'clock call came. He'd answered quickly, and Maura rolled over, sighing back into her dream.

He'd known all evening that the call would come. After Daisy died, Maura shifted their evening walk to avoid a baby-clothing store. But this evening, they'd resumed their old route, Maura even glancing at the pale green onesie in the window, and Adam knew. Daisy was telling him it was time.

When they did try again, Adam hoped for a boy. Not that he preferred a son. He just couldn't bear to use Daisy's pink "I'm An Angel" sweater for another child.

Another child. That thought roiled his stomach and scattered his thoughts. No baby could replace Daisy. Yet he yearned to be a family man, a gift only a future baby could provide.

But that was for another time. Tonight, Daisy was giving him her last gift.

A lurch flung Adam sideways, smacking his cheek against the window, and banging his elbow against the cabin wall. Something behind him jiggled.

The helicopter resumed a level posture.

Adam rubbed the sting from his cheek and pressed the headset button. "Maybe we should have taken a plane instead? It's pretty windy tonight for a helicopter." He had to get that heart.

"A small plane would have the same problem. Don't worry. We'll get you there."

"You're right." He'd questioned an expert on his machine. "Sorry."

Adam leaned into the cradle of his seat, taking pleasure in the rumble of the engine bringing him closer to Susanna's heart. To Daisy's gift.

He hadn't told Susanna's family about Daisy, whose entire three-day life was spent in his hospital. If she'd lived, she'd be almost the same age as Susanna, with a smile just as spectacular. But a street thug's punch to Maura's stomach had doomed her before she was born. Daisy had fought hard, fueled by a heart that was strong and pure, but half-formed lungs left her gasping for breath that never came.

Fritz yelled into the cockpit. "Are you on duty all night? Or did someone wake you, too?"

The pilot flicked a switch on his headset. "On call. Same as you."

The clouds were now so thick they obscured everything. The ghostly companion had enveloped them. The lack of a reference point made Adam slightly dizzy.

"I can't see!" Fritz scooted to the edge of his seat. "Is it safe to fly when you can't see?" He clutched his stomach. "I'm getting dizzy."

"They know what they're doing," Adam said. Fritz questioned Adam's decisions with as little reason, but chastising him was like yelling at a puppy. Fritz would just stare back with big eyes and no clue what he'd done wrong.

"We'll rely on instruments," the co-pilot said.

"Instruments can't tell if you're about to fly into a mountain or a power line," Fritz said. He doubled over and stuck his head between his knees.

"Yes, they can. Every instrument works together." The co-pilot pulled a lever. "Moving the cyclic forward drops the nose, losing altitude and increasing airspeed, while moving it back slows her and makes us climb. Coordinating the two lets you change airspeed while maintaining altitude."

Adam nodded. Push and pull, that was how life worked. Yin and yang. Seemingly opposite forces depended on each other; shadows only existed where there was light. Transplanting a viable heart into an ailing patient, seeing that patient thrive and witnessing the family's elation—those moments were why Adam had chosen transplant surgery. But that heart came at a cost. Every positive brought an offsetting negative.

"I feel like we're about to crash," Fritz yelled. Adam was experiencing the same sensation, but he knew not to believe it.

The co-pilot tapped the altitude meter. "This tells us we're moving straight ahead. Don't pay attention to gut feelings. Your body plays tricks on you when you can't see the horizon. Trust the instruments."

Adam nearly reminded Fritz that trusting the people and equipment around him was a good idea in most situations, but a retching sound stopped him. Fritz was vomiting into his paper bag. Adam would smell donut mush the rest of the trip.

"Want to take a selfie?" Adam muttered.

Fritz moaned and squished his cheek against the window. As Adam closed his eyes to block out the disorientation and dizziness the clouds brought, the smell of the co-pilot's hot chocolate sent Adam's mind zooming back to the worst week of his life. After Daisy died, a nurse had thrust a Styrofoam cup of hot chocolate at him. He'd used it as a shield against the torrent of hugs.

The street thug turned out to be a short, skinny kid named Lonneman, a/k/a Lonnie. After he mugged another woman, Maura's line-up identification helped the prosecutor negotiate a better plea deal. Daisy didn't get any say at all. The plea bargain gave Lonneman just a few months in jail, and even that only because he'd slipped over the cusp of adulthood a few days before the mugging.

Adam could picture Daisy's childhood almost as if it had actually happened, leaving a framed photo memory angled on their mantel, with Daisy riding piggyback on his shoulders as he walked along the strip of wet where sand became wave, and then sand again. A seagull's squawk sent her into giggle fits and she cupped his chin for support. Her snub nose was her mother's and her skin too, pale and freckled. But her deep brown eyes and thicket of dark lashes were his. She was like a jigsaw puzzle of a sunset, where the pieces nestling in harmony formed a beauty you just had to stop to gaze at.

"Annie's coming to visit this weekend," Fritz said.

Adam turned his back to Fritz and scrolled through email, his screen bright against the dark cabin. The words zooming up his screen blurred into black and white Rorschach images that became a series of pictures, all of Daisy, as if each year's photos were stored in their own folder. Lonneman hadn't just killed Daisy, he'd killed all the future Daisys. A fresh victim arrived each year. Adam couldn't imagine living through the year of Daisy the bride.

"Annie and her mother are planning the wedding," Fritz said. "That's all they talk about. Flowers, photographs, they argue over every little detail." He was quiet for a moment, giving Adam a spark of hope before he said, "Annie's mother is already asking when we plan on having kids."

Adam's stomach flung his bite of donut halfway back up his throat, along with a bitter, oniony coating.

Fritz babbled on. "Annie and I are planning on two kids, but her mother wants a whole houseful of runny noses."

Adam leaned against the headrest and swallowed the bile.

"Are you all right, Dr. Porter? You don't look so good."

He opened one eye to glance at Fritz. "I haven't thrown up yet."

Fritz's phone balanced precariously on a tapping knee. "Annie and I want two kids, a boy and a girl."

"You don't get to choose whether you have a boy or a girl." You didn't even get to choose if your child lived.

"Well, hopefully, we'll have one of each." Fritz scrunched pudgy cheeks. "Though I guess it's easier if you have two boys or two girls. You can re-use all the clothes and toys you get from baby showers."

Adam's fingers tingled with the itch to use Fritz's cheeks as a punching bag. Daisy's angel sweater still sat in a corner of their unfinished basement.

"I have two girls and, believe me, it's not easier," the co-pilot said. "They're not even teenagers yet and already boys are calling."

Fritz chuckled. "You have to watch out for teenage boys."

"Shit," the pilot said. "GPS just went out. The air base must be jamming the signal for training."

"Why would they do that?" Fritz yelped. "They'll make us crash."

"It's four in the morning," Adam said. "It's not like the sky is flooded with traffic." He glanced out the window. They'd dropped below the clouds, the ghost's departure revealing scattered lights below, with the brighter Milky Way of the city just ahead.

"How will you get there without GPS?" Fritz asked the co-pilot. "Can you see the hospital?"

"Not yet, but we'll fly by dead reckoning until then."

"Dead reckoning?"

"We pick a position, or a fix, and advance that based on flight speed, wind, course and time. We adjust as we go." The co-pilot flicked a glance back at Fritz. "Dead reckoning was the first form of navigation and it worked pretty well."

"It's basically the opposite of instrument flying," Adam told him. Push and pull.

The constellation of lights grew closer. Within the cluster, a trickle of cars paraded headlights between dark buildings with a sprinkling of bright squares. The air force base to the north had its own light cluster, bordered by the black of the ocean. Adam caught a glimpse of the hospital roof's landing pad. A smile settled in his stomach.

Susanna's heart beat in that building.

"I hope we get that heart in time," Fritz said. Adam looked over, surprised. Fritz's voice had sounded as if it had come from his own thoughts. Fritz added, "I'd hate to think that poor little girl will die."

"Susanna's not a poor little girl." Adam had hated the looks the other doctors and the nurses gave him when Daisy died, their faces flooded with pity. He'd lost his status as a colleague when he became a grieving father. Worse, a grieving doctor who couldn't save his own child.

"Don't pity her, Fritz." Adam closed his eyes.

When he opened his eyes again, the helicopter was lowering toward the hospital.

A gust slammed Adam into the wall. He grabbed his seat cushion and ordered his mind to think of something else. Anything else.

Maura had just picked up red velvet cupcakes for their anniversary. She'd made a red velvet cake on their first date, and it became an anniversary staple. Adam didn't really like red velvet cake, but he loved that tradition.

Lonneman had attacked Maura from behind, knocking her down and spilling the cupcakes onto the damp sidewalk. When he tried to grab her purse, she didn't let go, so he punched her in the stomach, right where her bulge was biggest. Adam didn't see Maura until the hospital, but he imagined red velvet cake dissolving into the wet sidewalk, the sweet cupcakes unable to stay in one piece. Like Daisy.

The wind subsided, the helicopter steadied and they dropped toward the roof. The last time Adam had landed at this hospital, barely a week earlier, had been Brian's final trip. They'd finished the operation and were waiting in the physician's lounge for paperwork, with Adam and another doctor comparing residency experiences, when a nurse poked her head in.

She told the other doctor, "Lonneman's taken a turn for the worse. His PTT is 57. What do you want to do with the drip? He's in Room 323 now."

"I'll check on him." The doctor jogged out the door.

Adam waited until the doctor walked past the lounge again before mumbling something about the restroom, and heading for Room 323. He almost hoped for a different Lonneman, maybe an old man whose obesity had finally gotten the best of him.

But even in sleep, his trademark smirk lingered, his eyes closed tight under thick lashes. The hospital gown dwarfed his body, its short sleeves draping over skinny arms. The fist that had uprooted Adam's family tree was taped with an IV port.

Adam leaned over and examined Lonneman's face, selecting his long nose as the bull's eye for his knuckles. He cocked both fists, his arms shaking in anticipation.

In the pause before Adam struck, the beeping monitor broadcast the steadiness of the patient's heart.

Adam dropped his hands and shook the tremble from his arms. He tilted his head back to focus on a crack in a ceiling tile, a trick he often used to clear his mind. He stared at the pebbly tile and listened to the steady beep. Thump, thump, thump. Each beat hitting at precisely the same interval. A perfect performance.

He felt a surge of pure joy. Daisy had had her say after all. This was how she wanted it. Push and pull, opposite forces feeding each other. Adam smiled as he pictured Susanna in her hospital bed, with the same pug nose and freckles Daisy would've had. Freckles that were meant to grow old, along with their owner.

Susanna's father would get to walk along the beach with his daughter.

Adam looked around the room. Lonneman's room was smaller than Susanna's, with wooden visitor chairs instead of a love seat, and walls painted long ago. Yet some things were the same: the monitors, the railing on the bed, the hum of activity just outside the door. In its essence, one room could be swapped for the other.

Adam scanned Lonneman's chart, lingering on blood type and medical history, before reading the diagnosis. Pulmonary embolism. A blood clot damaging the lungs. Lonneman's lungs were failing him, just as Daisy's had failed her. The chart indicated multiple injuries, probably from a victim who'd gotten in a punch of his own.

He pressed a finger on Lonneman's wrist, feeling like a concertgoer snagging a swipe of a rock star arm, actually touching the person who had dominated his life. The heartbeat pulsed against Adam's finger, sending warm prickles of affection through him. He wanted to embrace the Lonneman heart, to feel it beat against his cheek like a cat's purr. The heart Daisy had sent him.

Adam lifted his hand, and turned to the IV tube and bag that dripped Heparin into the patient. He typed numbers into the monitor, changing the drip rate. Lonneman would get a lot more Heparin now. The machine beeped to acknowledge his instruction to do more of what it was designed to do.

Adam squeezed the bag, even though he knew it wouldn't affect the drip rate. If the liquid were a fist, his revenge would be perfect, a punch to the gut that stopped the lungs without hurting the heart. It might take a few days for the lungs to go, but once they did, the heart could depart for a new body. And this heart was strong. Perfect. Regardless of the drip rate, that dutiful organ would produce thump after thump, steady and true, despite the failings of the body in which it resided. And when it reached its rightful place, that heart would thump for decades, a loyal drummer in service to a deserving master.

Adam returned to the physician's lounge in time for a cup of weak coffee before a security guard with a bowling ball belly escorted them to the helicopter.

That same guard watched now as the helicopter approached the hospital roof. The guard made eye contact with Adam before the wind whipped the helicopter toward a construction crane. Adam glimpsed the nuts and bolts along the crane's spine as they skirted it. Fritz's face paled and he squeezed his eyes shut. Adam closed his eyes too. He needed that heart. Daisy was counting on him.

When Adam opened his eyes, they were landing with a gentle tiptoe on the roof. Adam and Fritz followed the guard to the operating room. As they waited for the transplant paperwork, Adam sent a silent thank-you to Daisy for this last reminder of her, a reminder that would pulse on and on, for all those years she'd been denied.

An orderly wheeled the donor in and placed him with his chest directly underneath a cluster of bright lights. A nurse checked the monitors while the surgical team took positions around Lonneman's body.

The nurse tapped her phone. "You like classic rock, right, Dr. Porter? Playlist one?"

"Let's go with playlist two this time."

"Guns N' Roses, it is."

As the opening riff of "Sweet Child O' Mine" rippled through the operating room, Adam Porter poised his scalpel above the body that held Susanna's heart.

✗

Leone Ciporin's short stories have appeared in *The Saturday Evening Post, Woman's World,* and *Mystery Weekly*, as well as numerous anthologies. She's a member of Mystery Writers of America and Sisters in Crime. When she's not writing short stories, Leone works as a manager in an insurance company's law department, which is more interesting than it sounds. Leone lives in Charlottesville, Va.

THE MAN FROM TOPEKA
ROBERT LOPRESTI

"How long have these parties been going on?" Matt asked.

"Let me think," said Larry. He sipped a martini to lubricate his brain cells. "This is the *summer* dinner so we started, um, nearly four years ago."

"And there are four parties a year," said Matt. He was tall and handsome, in an annoying way. Worse, his glass appeared to be full of club soda.

"The Goldbergs started them," Larry explained. He pointed at Carl and Janet, both bespectacled and leaning toward plump. They had been the last to arrive and were chatting with Don and Bev Falber, who were hosting this event.

"They thought the neighbors should get to know each other better and suggested that we hold seasonal dinners."

"Seems like a great idea," said Matt.

Larry nodded. "The hard part was coming up with five couples who were interested and would fit in."

"Why five?"

"Had to be an odd number. If it were four the same couple would make the winter dinner every year, and so on."

"I get it. Well, I'm glad Irene invited me."

Unlike the others who would be dining at the Falbers' that night, Matt didn't live in the neighborhood.

Larry tried to remember how long Irene's most recent boyfriend had lasted. Two dinners? Maybe three? That guy possessed a truly obnoxious laugh, but at least he had the decency to drink alcohol.

Larry wondered if Irene ever took up with a man just to have someone to bring to the dinner parties. She certainly hadn't missed any.

"We're glad you're here too," he said. "Where are you from originally, by the way?"

"Kansas."

"Yeah?" Larry brightened. "What part?"

"Topeka."

"I *love* Topeka. Spent most of a year there a while back. Met my wife there." Matt finished his drink. "Oh. Is she a native?"

"Nope. She was a newcomer, too. Her family moved there from Indiana while she was in college. We explored the place together. Say, what neighborhood did you live in?"

"Oh, all over. Hey, did I hear Nina say you're an architect?"

"Me?" Larry blinked. "No, I'm an investor."

"Ah. You run a hedge fund or something?"

He laughed. "Nothing that exciting. I just handle my own money."

"That can't be easy in this economy."

"I've seen better times. But we aren't bankrupt yet."

"Glad to hear it. Any tips?"

"Sorry." Larry shook his head. "Gave that up years ago. I recommended a stock to a friend. He lost ten grand and never spoke to me again."

"Well, I guess I can understand that."

"Sure. Except my previous tip made him almost thirty."

"What have you done for me lately?" said Matt. "Human nature, I guess. I think we're being called to dinner."

* * * *

"There's something strange about Irene's boyfriend," Larry told his wife as they were getting ready for bed.

"There certainly is," said Nina. "Starting with the fact that she calls him a *boyfriend*. Thirty-five year old women don't have boyfriends, unless they're cradle robbers. They have lovers, partners, or significant others. What's wrong with *paramour*? There's a good old word."

"My my." He raised his eyebrows. "Better out than in, I suppose. Someone might think you were jealous."

"Of Irene? You must be kidding. Off the bed, Lucky." She lifted the white terrier and put him on the floor next to his brown companion. "Ever since Bernie left Irene she's been bouncing from one lover to the next. I can't imagine having to break in so many men on how to share a blanket properly."

"So that's why you hang on to me."

"One reason. Seriously, Irene is not an advertisement for living happily after your husband runs off. So you'd better stick around."

"I plan to. But we're getting off track. Do you know where Matt is from?"

"Not a clue."

"He told me he was from Topeka. But when I asked him about it he changed the subject."

"Well, that's no mystery. Irene probably warned him about the psalms you sing to the glories of Topeka."

"I don't sing psalms. I just liked the place. And I met the most wonderful woman in the world there."

"Flattery will get you nowhere, darling. I'm tired."

"So be it. But I don't think he knew Topeka from Tacoma."

"Just leave Matt alone. Let Irene be happy for a change. She'll probably replace him with a new model before the next dinner."

* * * *

But Matt showed up at the Goldbergs' for the autumn party. When Larry spotted him he had a hot cider in his hand and was admiring a jack-o'-lantern carved to resemble a certain politician, not in a good way.

"Good to see you again, Larry."

"I've been seeing *you* most mornings. Driving by while I'm walking the dogs."

"Oh," said Matt. "Yes, I moved in with Irene in September."

"Congratulations. Say, what's that I smell from the kitchen?"

"Stuffed squash, I think."

Larry's eyes widened. "That's not the main course? Janet hasn't gone vegetarian on us, has she?"

Matt laughed. "I believe there's a chicken in the works for you carnivores."

No booze and no meat. The man was a sheer joy.

And that made Larry think: *No Topeka?*

"Vegetables are all right in their place, I guess. And speaking of place, I wanted to talk to you about beautiful Topeka. Where did you say you lived when you were there?"

Matt stared at his mug as if his hot cider had turned sour. "Oh, we spent some time in Ward Meade. And then we moved over by Hi-Crest."

"That's near Dornwood Park. I loved that park. Used to walk there often. Which high school did you go to?"

A scowl. "What is this? An inquisition?"

Irene and Nina appeared. Irene grabbed Matt's arm like he was a trophy she had just won. "What are you boys up to?"

Matt smiled at her. "Larry was worried that this might be a vegetarian dinner."

Nina grinned. "Wouldn't hurt you to eat lower on the food chain occasionally, darling."

"Matt has been a vegetarian for years," said Irene. "And he's *very* healthy." She squeezed his arm.

Larry sighed. He was losing his appetite.

* * * *

"The man is definitely a phony," said Larry, as they walked home. "He had memorized the names of a few neighborhoods in Topeka but when I asked him which high school he attended he lost his temper. Do you know anyone who doesn't remember the name of their high school?"

"Maybe he was a drop-out, darling. Maybe he was a nerd and they stuffed him in lockers. What does it matter?"

"Matter? The man's living practically across the street from us, and he's there under false pretenses. Who knows what his real story is?"

Nina turned to stare at him. "What are you saying? That he's a whistle-blower in the witness protection program?"

"The people in that program aren't whistleblowers. Most of them are snitches who ratted out their fellow gangsters." He thought about it. "But they usually have a better cover story than Matt does."

"Cover story." Irene unlocked their door. "Darling, you've been watching too many spy movies."

Larry bent down to snatch Reno and Lucky as they scrabbled on the tile floor, each trying to be the first one out. "Well, how about this? Maybe he's a con man after Irene's money."

"Does she have any? She works in real estate, which is hardly the road to riches these days. I don't know what kind of divorce settlement she got from Bernie."

"Okay, okay. But why pretend to be from Kansas unless you have something to hide?"

* * * *

The winter dinner was always held at the end of January, slipped between the holiday madness and Valentine's Day.

Two days before the event Nina hung up the phone with a frown. "That was Irene with bad news. They won't be coming on Saturday. Matt has the flu."

Larry put down the remote. "I knew it."

"Knew what?"

"That he'd back out. The dinner is at our house and that faker realized I could control the seating. He wouldn't take the chance that I'd question him in front of Irene."

"If I thought you were going to grill *me* I wouldn't come either. But listen, darling. I just thought of another possibility."

"Yeah? What's that?"

She leaned over his chair, whispering like a conspirator. "Maybe he really *has* the flu. The same one that kept you on your back for a week."

"He's not sick, Nina. He's avoiding me. Well, let's see what he does about the April dinner. *They* are supposed to host that one."

* * * *

A week before the spring event Matt rang the doorbell. "Hi, neighbor. Can I come in for a minute?"

Larry hesitated, thinking about desperadoes silencing people who knew too much. For a moment he wished his terriers were German shepherds.

Then he looked out at the beautiful late March afternoon in gloriously green suburbia. How could anyone plot a murder among these manicured lawns?

"Come in. You want a drink?"

"I'll take a cola, if you have one."

"Coming right up. Have a seat. Nina's at her spinning class."

"I saw her go. I wanted to catch you alone. Listen." He sighed. "You know I'm not from Kansas."

"Oh." Larry looked at his beer bottle. "Well, I suspected it."

"Okay, you got me. But I'd appreciate it if you don't tell Irene."

"I can't promise that until you tell me why the deception."

"This is embarrassing," said Matt. "The fact is, I'm from Baltimore."

Larry waited but Matt said nothing else, just drank soda and looked as if he had revealed a great and guilty secret.

"Sorry, I don't get it. What's wrong with Baltimore?"

"Did you know Irene's ex-husband?"

"Bernie? Slightly. He left a few months after we moved here."

"Well, *he* was from Baltimore."

"Ah *ha*."

"Irene and I met on a dating site. Hit it off, so we had coffee. I invited her for dinner at a place that serves great shellfish. That's when it started."

Matt shook his head. "She said she never ate crabs because they reminded her of Baltimore. Started a rant about how Bernie left her, drove off in their brand new car and never came back."

"And she holds that against the whole city?"

"You have no idea. She loved Edgar Allan Poe in school, but she won't have his books in the house now because he used to live there."

"He's buried there, too, I think."

"Anyway, when she asked me where I was from, I panicked."

"And picked Topeka. Why?"

"I don't know. It sounded safe and far away. How could I know one of her neighbors was a native?"

"I'm not *from* Topeka. I just have fond memories of the place. So you're from Baltimore, huh?"

"Yup. Went to Southwestern High School. I probably still have my senior yearbook if you want proof."

"No, no. I'm convinced and your secret is safe with me." Larry sighed. "I admit I'm a little disappointed."

"Why is that?"

"I thought the explanation might be a little more dramatic." He sipped beer, and then smiled. "I don't suppose you being a vegetarian and a teetotaler is just an act, too?"

"Sorry. That's the real me."

"Oh, well."

* * * *

"Baltimore?" said Nina. "That's the big secret?"

"I'm afraid so," said Larry. He was washing dishes. She was drying. "A bit of a letdown, huh? Did you know Irene had a grudge against Charm City?"

"I know she didn't watch *The Wire*. But I thought she just hated cop shows." Nina shook her head. "I hope this will break you of the habit of talking about Topeka."

"You can't blame this on Topeka."

"Larry, I'm serious. What if someone asked what you were *doing* there?"

"What do you mean? I was on business."

"And if they kept asking questions?" Nina's voice dropped an octave. "Funny you should ask. I had just stolen a huge pile of securities from an eccentric lawyer in Mississippi. Spent six months in Topeka waiting for a man to launder the money. I wound up marrying the fence's daughter."

"Okay, I see your point."

"So that's why I love Topeka," she continued. "It's where I made enough money to go legit."

Larry raised his hands. "I surrender! I'll never mention Kansas again."

"Good. And no more prying into our neighbors' lives. You're the man on the run, after all."

"I'm *not* on the run. No one suspected me of anything. But okay, I'll shut up."

"One more thing," said Nina. She put down her towel. "Are you sure Irene said Bernie drove off in their new car?"

"That's what Matt said."

"But it's not true. I remember the day Irene told me Bernie had left. I noticed that both cars were still there and she said Bernie had taken a taxi to the airport. He had told her to sell the car and send him the money. We joked that she should do like the old urban legend—sell it for fifty bucks."

"Maybe he came back for the car."

"I don't think so." She frowned. "Has anybody heard from Bernie, since he left?"

"Well, I know I haven't."

"Irene hated her husband and he vanished. You don't suppose—"

"No, I don't," said Larry. "And *you* don't either. Like you said, we're through prying into our neighbors' lives. I'm sure that Bernie is fine. He's probably started a new life for himself—"

"In Topeka?"

Robert Lopresti is a retired librarian and the president of the Short Mystery Fiction Society. He is the author of two novels (most recently *Greenfellas*) and 80+ short stories. He is the winner of the Derringer Award (three times), the Black Orchid Novella Award, and the Lane/Saunders Memorial Research Award.

VICE COP

ELIZABETH ZELVIN

I cursed Spellcheck, Peewee Libitski, and the law—the first for turning my report into gibberish and the third for making me let the second go. Not enough evidence to charge him. Again. I would be late to drive Gracie to the mall. She was already mad at me because I insisted on escorting her. I wouldn't leave until her friends arrived, jailbait with downy cheeks and trusting eyes. It didn't embarrass Gracie that they dressed like prostitutes. She'd do the same if I let her. *I* embarrassed her. When she said her dad was a vice cop, they laughed. What a joke.

Peewee Libitski was no joke. I was sure he trolled for underage girls on the Internet. But Cybercrimes was so backed up I wasn't getting the cooperation I needed. A couple of girls with the wavy brown hair, blue eyes, and apple cheeks he liked were missing in nearby counties. I was convinced they were dead, thanks to Peewee. My bosses didn't buy it. I was waiting for him to make a date close to home.

What scared me was that Gracie was his type. I hoped my lectures had sunk in.

"These SOBs lie, Gracie. They're good at it. Don't get chummy with a stranger on Facebook just because she *says* she's a girl."

Exaggerated sigh and eye roll. I didn't know if the offense was "SOB," "chummy," "Facebook," or all three.

"Never give out your full name online."

"I'm not an idiot, Dad. I use a screen name."

"Don't say where you live or give your relatives' names. Don't say when you're at home or what time you go to school or when you're at the mall. You're a smart girl, Gracie. Don't give them anything that identifies you or lets them track your movements."

"I *am* a smart girl, Dad," she always said. "You don't have to lecture me."

* * * *

You know dads, Gracie texts.

[eye-roll emoji]

This girl isn't giving much away. If she is a girl. Gracie is trolling for Dad's elusive predator. Most kids spill TMI online. Most kids could benefit from Dad's lectures. Note to self: tell principal to invite Dad to address the school assembly. "Too Much Information Can Get You Killed." He'll be wildly popular. The kids will love his stories about pimps and hookers. That will teach Charise and Leni and Shonda not to laugh at vice cops. He's cute, too, though she'll never tell him.

Right, terminally boring, Gracie texts.

Let's see how mystery girl—her handle is Tinkerbell—does with big words and good spelling. She's heard most cyberpedophiles sprinkle a lot of BFFs and OMGs into their texts. To Gracie, it would be a dead giveaway. Their buzz words would be way behind. They wouldn't sound authentic. *She* would never fall for it. But Dad's hard-to-catch suspect may be smart enough to avoid it.

What does your dad do?

Ah, now Tinkerbell is participating in the conversation. If Gracie tells her he's a cop, will she vanish? Hmm, what kind of dad is boring?

Accountant. In love with numbers, like what time will I be home and how many drinks did I have at the party. Lucky I'm good at giving him the slip.

Clever Jinx.

Who? Oh, yeah, Gracie's own handle in this chat. She'd better remember it. There *is* something off about Tinkerbell. How many teens would use a word like "clever?"

How about yours? Gracie texts.

Dads a lawyer, moms a college professor...

careers keep them both so busy i can do whatever i want...

the only question they ask is do you need money

Dad says that when a witness gives you more information than you ask for, he's probably lying. Dad says you can learn a lot from lies. Lawyer and college professor—safe and respectable, meant to reassure her. Gracie—Jinx—has trouble getting away. But Tinkerbell can meet her any time, and she's got plenty of money—powerful lures to a teen on a short leash.

And Gracie would bet all the imaginary money Tink's imaginary parents give her against her own modest allowance that Tink is imaginary too, cover for a sex criminal her dad would give anything to bring to justice.

* * * *

Lloyd hated that nickname, Peewee, invented to torment him in the schoolyard. His type was girls who looked like Margie James, the girl he asked to the senior prom. She said no, and worse, she laughed at him. But he made sure her prom date's kiss on the doorstep was not the memory she took to bed that night.

Over the years, Libitski upped his game. Right now he had two on the hook. His cellar girl, Tinkerbell he called her, would do anything he told her to. And now this Jinx was in his sights. He'd met her in a chat room. She was dumb enough to post a photo. What was wrong with parents? Didn't they teach their daughters anything? It was their own fault they went missing and turned up dead.

* * * *

Gracie is convinced by now that Tinkerbell is Dad's predator. She still doesn't know his name, because Dad is too good a cop to tell her the name of anyone involved in an active investigation. But she knows this case is keeping him awake at night. And though you can see it kills him to tell her even a scrap of inside information, he says that for her own protection, he wants her to know that this particular joker has a type, girls who look like her. He means it to serve as a warning. It isn't his fault it acts more like catnip to a feisty kitten. Now she knows how to hook this crook. If she can hook him, she can reel him in. She *knows* it will be dangerous. *Of course* she'll bring Dad in before it gets too dangerous. But not quite yet.

Dad's told her about grooming in his vice cop voice. Sex offenders get innocent young girls comfortable by being nice at first, acting like uncles or brothers or genuine boyfriends they can fall in love with. Then harmless or cute but sexy private photos or videos lead to pornographic photos that find their way onto the Internet and can't be recalled. Sex with the groomer leads to sex with multiple partners who can't be refused. Niceness disappears. Instead, the girls may be subject to beatings and even murder. Gracie can imagine a girl getting suckered in. It chills her. But she wants to reassure her dad.

"Please don't worry," she says. "I get it. But if scaring people safe worked, would there be any crime?"

"Your point," he says, "is that people can't be scared safe, any more than they can be scared straight. But I'm your dad. It's my job to make sure you have the information. And to worry."

"You're the best dad on the planet." She flings her arms around him, pressing her head against his chest. "It wasn't fair of Mom to divorce you and move all the way across the country with that creep of a new boyfriend."

Her father strokes her hair.

"That's not fair, Gracie. The divorce was at least half my fault. You know what being a cop does to marriages. Maybe I'm not fit to raise a teenage daughter."

"You are! You are! You're the best, Dad, and I'll always love you!"

She almost confesses then and there. But won't he be happier if she helps him bring in the bad guy? And her plan will work, she knows it will.

* * * *

I knew Gracie was up to something. On the surface, nothing changed. She spent hours online. She met her friends at the mall. One of them turned sixteen, and I met the girl and gave permission for her to drive Gracie to the mall. Why did parents give sixteen-year-olds cars? Answer: they didn't see as many dead kids in the morgue as I did. If they were lucky, none.

At work, I was told to get my mind off Peewee Libitski, because he was only my problem if I caught him with enough evidence to prosecute on sex offenses. If another girl with brown hair, blue eyes, and rosy cheeks went missing, that was for Missing Persons, and if such a girl turned up dead, it was Homicide's case. So why didn't I go out and catch some pimps or, better, sex traffickers red-handed like a good vice cop or break up a pornography ring involving corrupt politicians and make the media happy. And while I was at it, stop pestering Cybercrimes. Their workload was big enough without special requests from me.

That didn't stop me from keeping an eye out for all the things they told me to ignore. I stayed under the radar as best I could. My contact in Missing Persons was an officer named Gladys who'd never sought promotion, gone gray at thirty-five, and acted like a mother hen to anyone who would let her, colleagues as well as the distraught relatives of people who unexpectedly disappeared. She made the best coffee in the station. It was my excuse to drop by every few days, asking about blue-eyed girls with brown hair and rosy cheeks.

When I arrived this time, Gladys was dispensing tea and sympathy to a troubled mother with a skinny blond girl who looked about twelve in tow. Gladys introduced me to her visitors as someone with a special concern for missing girls.

"I don't believe she's run away," the mother said. "Madeline is such a sensible girl. But I know all her friends, and none of them has seen her." She dabbed at her eyes with a wad of tissues.

"Not one of yours," Gladys told me over the mother's bent head, handing me a picture. "Brown eyes."

"What?" The blond girl sat up straight and reached out for the photo. "Mom! That's Maddy's class picture! She wore her brown contacts that day for a joke." Her gaze darted back and forth between Gladys and me. "My sister's eyes are blue."

"Sukey," the mother said, "don't talk out of turn. You're confused."

"I'm not confused!" Sukey said indignantly. "Ma, they're trying to *find* her! Don't waste time prettying things up!"

I jerked my head toward the door, indicating to Gladys that I'd like to talk to Sukey privately.

Gladys knelt beside the mother. She spoke in her most soothing tone.

"We will do everything we can to find your daughter."

Sukey followed me into the hall and closed the door.

"I can tell you things about Maddy," she said, "that my mom doesn't want to hear."

"Maddy's cheeks seem very rosy in the photo. Does she wear rouge?"

"No. Everyone always asks, but her cheeks are naturally rosy. She hates it."

"Do you think your sister has run away, or do you think something has happened to her?"

"I'm not sure," she said, "but I'm worried. What my mom said about knowing all Maddy's friends? She knows her school friends. But Maddy has online friends that Mom knows nothing about. There's this one friend Maddy's been talking to for weeks who's sort of a secret even from me."

"Sort of a secret?"

"I know her name is Tigerlily."

"Not a boy. Not a romance, then?"

"She's not a secret lesbian, if that's what you mean," Sukey said.

"Do you know if they talked about meeting in person?"

"Yes, but she wouldn't tell me any details. She said Tigerlily was afraid her parents would find out and stop her. They're very controlling. They have a lot of rules about who her friends are and how much time she spends on the Internet and what she's allowed to watch."

"Is Maddy the kind of girl who sticks up for the underdog?" I asked.

"Yes! How did you know?" Sukey was impressed. My powers of wizardry, kid. "Those parents made her mad. She really wanted to, you know, put some stuffing in Tigerlily."

"What do you think happened, Sukey?" I asked. "Does anything in particular bother you? Something you're afraid of? Something Maddy said?"

"No-o-o. But something must have gone wrong. Maybe Tigerlily didn't show up. But then why didn't Maddy come home? Or Tigerlily's parents threw her out, or there was an accident. I couldn't tell Mom or Dad any of this."

"We'll tell your parents ourselves," I said. "It wasn't your job to stop her. How come your dad isn't here today?"

"He's on a business trip. Mom hasn't told him yet that Maddy is missing."

"We'll take care of that," I said. "Does Maddy have a laptop?"

"Yes, but she took it with her," Sukey said. "And I've been calling and texting her for days. She never answers. Why can't she use her phone? She must have it on her. She'd rather die than be without her phone."

* * * *

Gracie agrees to meet Tinkerbell, saying her father insists on coming along. He likes to meet any new online friend before he trusts his daughter to spend time alone with her. If Tink is really a college girl, she won't mind. If she bails, she probably isn't. But even if she is a bad guy pretending to be a college girl, she has already invested a lot of time and effort in Gracie—as much as Gracie has invested in her.

I'm two minutes away, Gracie texts. *Dad parking car.*

Lies. Gracie keeps an eye on the empty tables for two at the fast food joint where they're supposed to meet. Her heart thumps at the thought that she may see the bad guy soon. She plans to remain in hiding, take a few quick pix on her phone, and get out fast. She'll text Tink with some excuse once she's safely away.

It will be a relief if no one comes. How long should she give it? Fifteen minutes? Twenty? And what next? Confess to Dad and let him talk her out of taking it any further?

A girl who might be Gracie's age but walks without Gracie's swagger comes in. She sits at one of the small tables. This is an unexpected contingency. Gracie throws her shoulders back and approaches the girl, who is twisting a paper napkin from the dispenser.

"Are you Tinkerbell?"

The girl looks startled. Her hair is the same soft brown as Gracie's, her eyes as blue, her cheeks as rosy. It's like looking in a mirror for both of them.

"Yes. Jinx?"

"My dad just texted," Gracie says. "He's parked now, but he needs to do some shopping. He'll meet me at the Security booth at the mall entrance in half an hour. And if I know Dad, he'll raise hell if I'm not there on time."

That should keep her safe. Not that the girl seems dangerous. She's scared, not at all like the Tink from the online chats. She stares past Gracie's shoulder.

Maybe the bad guy is watching. Too bad Dad isn't really waiting at the Security booth.

Tinkerbell doesn't have much to say. If Gracie chatters, she may give too much away. She'd better ask some questions.

"So you want to major in English? What courses are you taking?"

The girl looks relieved. She tells Gracie what books she's reading for her nineteenth-century English lit course. They both like *Jane Eyre* better than *Wuthering Heights* and Jane Austen better than both the Brontës put together. Tinkerbell seems to relax. Once she almost laughs.

Then Gracie says, "Online, when I mentioned Helen Burns as Jane's BFF, you didn't seem to know who I was talking about."

"Oh, no, you must be mistaken. I knew you meant Jane Eyre's friend who died at that awful school. *Please* don't mention it again."

She grabs Gracie's hand across the table. Tink's is clammy and trembling.

"Promise me," she says.

"I promise," Gracie says. "Already forgotten."

Tinkerbell knows her *Jane Eyre*, but the bad guy has never read it. He's keeping Tink alive to tell him how to talk to her, Gracie. And Tink made a mistake, didn't give him a fact he needed. What has he done to her that she is so scared of one small failure coming up again?

"Are you in trouble?" Gracie says. "Let me help."

"No," Tink says, "nobody can help. You don't understand."

"Try me," Gracie says, "Don't worry"—as the girl rears back like a nervous horse—"forget it. Let's just smile and act normal. We talked about books, it was nice, and everything's okay."

"Oh!" the girl says. "I'm supposed to—that is, we talked about my reading your writing."

"Yes, a story," Gracie says. "I didn't bring it this time. Let's make another date."

"Not now," the girl says. "You—we can make another date online. Here again? It's supposed—it's best in about a week." Her voice trembles. "I hope I'll be here."

"I hope you will too," Gracie says.

* * * *

When Gracie told me she'd been chatting with Peewee Libitski—*probably*, Dad—and worse, agreed to meet him on her own, I wanted to wring her neck. All my warnings only inspired her to sail right into the midst of danger.

"My God, Gracie," I said, "I thought you had some common sense."

"I do have common sense, Dad," she said. "That's why I'm *telling* you. I *did* meet a girl who's read Jane Austen and the Brontës. Tinkerbell still could be a college girl who wants to mentor a high school girl with a good vocabulary who wants to be a writer."

"You want to be a writer?" I was momentarily distracted.

"Da-ad. The point is I don't think she is. If she's not his prisoner, why should she be scared?"

I groaned and clutched at my face with my hands. For once I was glad her mother was on the other side of the country.

"Dad, give me some credit. I was going to meet her two more times before I told you, and I didn't."

"You think I'd—"

"*Listen*! I thought I'd give her the story in a day or two, and we'd meet again a couple of days later to discuss it. By then, I'd be sure, and she would trust me. But then she said a week, and I could tell it wasn't her own idea. Dad, I felt really scared! And not like when you're really little and you see *The Wizard of Oz* for the first time."

That made me laugh.

"You were five. You were scared of the Wicked Witch and adorable in your little pumpkin pajamas."

"That's what I mean," she said. "This wasn't like that. It was pure dread, the real thing. Not for me, for her. Dad, if he has a week, he'll kill her before he snatches me."

"You don't leave me much choice," I said.

"Dad, if you saw her!" she said. "She's terrified, and she looks so much like me!"

"That's another thing," I said. "How did he find you? Did he stalk you? Does he know where you live?"

"Don't underestimate me, Daddy," she said. "I knew you wouldn't want me to be stalked, and you'd hate it if he knew our address. So I cut through all that. I posted a photo."

"Good God Almighty! What did I do wrong?"

"Nothing! You raised a daughter who's going to help you get this guy so he can't hurt any more girls like me. You're smarter than him, but you haven't given him the right b— incentive."

She was smart too. She knew if she'd said "bait," I would have lost it. Maybe locked her up until she turned twenty-five.

But she was right. It was my job to deliver Peewee Libitski to the stern embrace of the law. But returning Madeline to her family, making sure there were no more Madelines—that mattered. God help me, I was in.

"You know I'll probably get canned for this," I said. "I'll end up in a homeless shelter eating cat food, and you'll have to go and live with your mom."

I didn't point out that if I died keeping Gracie safe, she'd also have to go live with her mom. Cops and fathers did whatever it took.

* * * *

Now that Dad is involved, Gracie is no longer running the show. On the plus side, it makes her feel safer. A whole team will be on hand for the takedown. Dad has stopped moaning about what she's done and started treating her a bit like a grownup. As part of the team, she knows the bad guy's name now: Peewee Libitski. She'll wear a wire to the meet. If everything works out, she may have to testify. Dad patiently explains everything the police are supposed to do and not do to make sure the case stands up in court.

Gracie's most important job is to make contact again with the girl she's identified as the missing Madeline Halley, first from formal school photos in a lineup and then from family snapshots. Meeting her mother and sister makes Maddy herself more real. For the rescue not to succeed has become unthinkable. Maddy isn't in college yet, but she's been accepted and is planning to major in English. Peewee is very clever to have abducted someone who is his type and also fits the persona he's adopted to groom Gracie, all because Gracie talked about books and said she wanted to be a writer. If he didn't need her to disarm Gracie, Maddy might be dead already.

Gracie and the guy from Cybercrimes do not see eye to eye about teenagers' texting vocabulary. Dad mentions Gracie's sound instincts and points out how well she's already messed with Libitski's head. Cybercrimes, who looks like he lives in his parents' basement, eats nothing but Cheetos, and never reads a book, is skeptical. Dad says when you work with a team, there are always some decisions you may not like. He also says the police force has a chain of command, like the military.

"You're at the bottom of this chain, Gracie," he says. "If *anyone* on the team says, 'Run!' you run *at once*. If they say, 'Drop!' you hit the floor. You don't ask, 'Why?' or look around to see what's going on."

The way he says it scares her.

"I get it, Dad," she says. "I just do it."

"I want you coming out of this alive, Gracie," he says.

He sounds scared himself. And Dad is never scared. Never.

"If anything happens to you," he says, "your mother will kill me. And she'd hate prison. It's not half as nice as California."

She knows he's only joking so they can pretend the both of them aren't scared silly.

"Don't worry, Dad," she says, "I'll obey orders."

She texts Tinkerbell that her family is going away in a few days. They use her idea of saying how much she wants Tink to read her story and critique it so she can work on it while she's away. Cybercrimes waters "critique" down to "make suggestions." To make sure that Peewee sends Maddy again, Gracie texts that this time her dad will join them for sure. Meanwhile cops from the team will stake out the parking garage well in advance. They'll identify Peewee's car and plant a tracking device on it if Peewee leaves it unattended for long enough.

Peewee may stay in the car the whole time, so Gracie still needs to tell Maddy she is being rescued. She is supposed to give Maddy a second tracking device to conceal in Peewee's car while she and Peewee are driving back to his place.

There are so many catches in this that Gracie doesn't know which to worry about first. Maddy needs to trust Gracie. She needs to want to be rescued, too. She may have gotten attached to Peewee—Stockholm syndrome, that's it. She may not believe he'll kill her. On the other hand, she may want to be saved but be too scared of Peewee to take the tracker. Or what if Peewee sees Gracie hand Maddy the tracker? What will he do to Maddy when they're alone?

Gracie will be wired, so the team can hear what she says. What if Peewee wires Maddy up too? If he hears their conversation, he'll be angry, especially at Gracie for ruining his nice murder. What will he do, not only to Maddy but to Gracie if he gets hold of her? Will he have a gun? A knife? What *does* he do to those girls who look like her and Maddy? Dad won't tell her.

* * * *

My heart was in my mouth the whole time Gracie was out there. But the operation went well, if you could call it that when the brass of four different units—Vice, Missing Persons, Cybercrimes, and Homicide—couldn't stop squabbling about who was in charge and the alleged sex offender, kidnapper, cybercriminal, and maybe murderer managed to lose the unmarked police cars on his tail as he drove back to the unidentified location we needed to find.

Gracie did better than any of us. The fifteen-year-old trusted her, though she would tell my daughter no more than, "He hurt me so bad," in a broken whisper. And Maddy was too terrified to take a tracking device, sure that her captor would instantly know. Gracie got her to confirm he'd threatened to kill her sister. She believed he could do it any time, no matter how many assurances Gracie gave her that the police could and would protect Maddy's whole family.

I was just as glad Gracie didn't give the Halley girl a tracker. If Peewee found out, he would hold it against her. Gracie was already way more involved than I wanted her to be. At least Maddy wasn't wired for sound. Peewee still thought Jinx was an aspiring young writer. She'd written a sweet story— remember it's *fiction*, Dad. The heroine—*protagonist*, Dad—is a girl whose mother leaves for greener pastures while her accountant father tries to protect her from the world he fears will hurt her. Then she meets an older girl who has the kind of freedom she's always dreamed of. Ye gods, she made the accountant's daughter sound real. Was it her or wasn't it? I was afraid to ask. I wasn't a stupidly permissive dad, but I didn't think I was overprotective. Look at how I'd let her into this case.

"We have more important things to think about, Dad," Gracie said.

As if I didn't know! She was thinking like a cop. It made my gut clench, though I felt proud of her too.

"This next time has to be soon," she said, "like tomorrow, before he has time to kill Maddy."

"He thinks he's got five days," I said. "What if he says, 'What's the rush?'"

"I'll tell him my dad said I have to check the story critique off my to-do list right away so I can focus on the trip we're supposed to be taking. And Dad, Peewee's got to come to meet me himself, or it's all for nothing. Jinx's dad *said* he was coming twice and didn't show up. And I was fine alone with Tinkerbell at the mall. So I can tell her that my dad's relented. He doesn't need to come with me next time."

The brass agreed with Gracie. The only way to make Peewee show himself was to tell him in advance that Jinx would come alone.

* * * *

If she ever writes a TV cop show, Gracie thinks, she must remember that it isn't what you anticipate that goes wrong, but things you never thought of. Gracie is hardly seated when the sophisticated sound system that links her with her backup cuts out. She hopes they're watching, because the little man who's just arrived is Peewee Libitski. Both girls leap out of their chairs.

"This is my f-father," Maddy says. She sounds ready to keel over from sheer nerves.

"You're still supposed to call me Daddy, sweet girl."

"S-sorry, Daddy." Maddy hangs her head.

Holding out his hand to Gracie, he says, "You shall call me Mr. Libbey—with an 'e.'"

The hand is cold and limp. Grasp the hand firmly or match the limpness? Neither—he pulls the hand out of her grip and runs it lightly up the inside of her forearm.

"Nice," he says. "Smooth skin."

The man is truly creepy. He elongates his vowels and hisses his sibilants, as if he were speaking Parseltongue, like the snake in *Harry Potter*. Does the light touch on her arm count as a Me Too moment? She's been told the cops can't come charging out until they see him committing a crime.

"I can tell you didn't expect to see me." Drawn-out *e*'s, hissing *s*'s.

His eyes narrow into slits, while his grin and nostrils widen, making him look more than ever like a snake. Gracie can imagine a slim black forked tongue flicking in and out.

He *doesn't* know her thoughts and feelings. Saying he can tell is a trick to throw her off balance. He's just a little man in glasses, going bald, a head shorter than her dad. She'll be taller than Peewee herself when she grows up. And she *did* expect him. The glitch in the wire is the bad surprise.

"Hi, Mr. Libbey," she says.

Beside her, Gracie can feel Maddy quivering.

"Come with me, girls," he says, jovial as a Santa Claus who won't take no for an answer. "I'm going to buy you a couple of ice cream cones. You'll like that."

Peewee picks up Maddy's windbreaker and hands Gracie her things.

"Wait!" Gracie says. "What about my story? We were going to sit here and discuss it."

"My noodleheaded daughter forgot to bring it," he says. "Change of plans. It'll be okay. Mustn't crush the budding writer's career before she's even exssspeeerienssssed anything. Ice cream first."

It isn't a crime to buy your daughter and her friend an ice cream cone. Since the team can't hear her, she can't warn them Peewee is taking them away from the focus of their surveillance. Their route winds through the mall, around corners and through doors. They go in and out of shops, not stopping long enough even to browse, farther and farther from the fast food place. But Dad won't let her out of his sight. Whatever orders they give him, he'll follow her. Won't he?

Peewee watches them, unblinking, as they eat their ice cream cones. He chomps his own cone in fierce vertical movements of his front teeth like a nut-cracker doll, his tongue flicking out to catch an occasional trickle of melting ice cream.

Right across the way from the ice cream stand is a ladies room, the entrance discreetly concealed by a freestanding screening wall.

"I need to pee," Gracie says. "Tink, you must be bursting too. That was a big soda you were finishing when I got here."

If Maddy has an ounce of sense, she'll say she needs to go too. Now is the time for her to show some backbone. He can't follow them into the Ladies, can he?

* * * *

The one time I didn't need an excuse to be delayed getting to the mall, I really was held up in traffic. It was the kind of jam where all the whirling lights and sirens in the world don't help. The cars were packed solid eight lanes across and bumper to bumper for a mile. And my little girl was out there, going head to head with a killer.

We had agreed to keep the two-way silent as long as possible. The first thing the team said when I finally reached them on my cell was not reassuring.

"Has she called you?"

"You're supposed to be monitoring her every second. She's not supposed to need to call me. *Goddammit, have you lost my daughter?*"

"Keep your shirt on. The situation is under control. Where are you?"

I gave him the coordinates fast.

"What the hell happened?" I snapped.

Under control, my ass. They only said that when the situation was hopelessly out of control. *I* was under control. I made them tell me the truth with a temper tantrum I judged to the millimeter.

They'd lost audio contact with Gracie right after she'd arrived, but it was "temporary," and they were "working on it." Peewee was in their sights. The kidnapped girl was there. She was still alive. Wasn't that good news?

No! My baby was in danger, and I wasn't there! Until they got the system up and running, they were stuck with visual surveillance and cell phone contact. Wait, call coming in now. Not so good, but you gotta accept some setbacks, we'll get past this one.

"Goddammit, you *have* lost her!"

"Calm down, man, you're still on duty, and we need you fit for it. Take a deep breath. Get out of the car, see what's causing the holdup and if Traffic is on top of it. If you can't help them unsnarl it fast, see if they can help extract you from it." He added drily, "And if you can't remember your rank, remember mine."

"Yes, sir."

He had a point. Screaming and cursing at my boss's boss was a brief and potentially costly pleasure that did nothing to help Gracie. The fact that he was on the scene meant they were taking this operation very seriously.

"We did manage to get a tracking device onto Libitski's car. If your girl does call, tell her to throw hers away as soon as she gets the chance. If she's handed it off to the Halley girl, make sure she warns her to do the same."

"If we can follow Libitski, can't we extract the girls now, sir?" I asked.

"You know better than that, son," he said.

Yeah, I did, but I had to ask.

"He's highly efficient at cleaning up his crime scenes," he said. "He may do the same at home or wherever he stashes the girls and his mementos every time he goes out. You know what I'm going to say next."

I was, and I didn't want to hear it. They needed Gracie as well as Maddy to get into the car with him. They needed to apprehend him assaulting the girls— please God, only *starting* to assault the girls. Gracie needed to be brave enough and strong enough to fend him off until I got there.

"Sir! Call coming in on my cell, gotta go. It's her! Gracie! Gracie! My God, Gracie!"

"Daddy! Listen!" she said sharply. "Maddy's okay so far, we're in the Ladies. The sound went out, Daddy, the team couldn't hear anything we said."

"I know, honey."

"You're there? You followed us through the mall? I want you to find me *soon*!"

"I'm in traffic, but I'm on my way—"

"Oh, Daddy! What should we do?"

"I'm in touch with the team. They got a tracker onto the car. Throw yours in the toilet *now*! Maddy's too. Go on, let me hear it flush."

"Done. What next?"

I hated this, but what a good sport my Gracie was.

"We need you to get in the car with him. With the tracker, they'll be right behind you, and so will I."

"Can I get Maddy out the window?"

"No, honey, it has to be both of you. He can't suspect anything until we get to his place."

"Okay, Daddy. I wouldn't let Maddy be alone with him again, and she probably wouldn't let me either. At least we have a little breathing time. He can't come in the Ladies!"

Oh, my sweet child. She thought Ladies was a commandment, sacred, like Thou Shalt Not Kill.

Gracie shrieked.

"Dad! He just called, 'Girls! I'm coming in!'"

"Get in a stall. Pretend you got your period. Come out as if it was just a long bathroom break. I love you, sweetheart."

My brain finally started working. The key to beating a traffic jam was to abandon the car. Once Traffic understood the urgency, they helped me clamber over barriers and strands of wire to an uncrowded side street, where a beautiful police car waited for me. The team not only picked up the tracking device on Peewee's car, they also fixed Gracie's wire. High time. I was closer to our quarry, so I didn't wait for the team. I tore through the streets with red lights whirling and siren howling until I got close to Peewee's place, where stealth made more sense.

I busted the lock quietly. It's a trick we have in Vice. Narcotics are the kickers in of doors. Peewee clearly didn't expect to be disturbed. The girls were posed against a backdrop that could have been a stage set, clad in costumes that might have shocked me if I didn't see Gracie and her friends at the beach every summer. They were locked in place, so his lawyers couldn't argue that it was voluntary. I won't say any more about the evidence of his intentions, except that Maddy showed clear signs of rough handling from the week she'd already spent in Peewee's hands. He was fiddling with one of those old-fashioned tripod cameras with big plates, his head underneath the black cloth. It would have been an uneventful collar if Gracie hadn't been so glad to see me.

"Daddy!" she shrieked.

Peewee's head popped out from underneath the cloth. I expected him to make a run for it or else face off with me. I outweighed him by fifty pounds and topped him by close to a foot. I was ready for either move. But damned if he didn't rush around and fling himself in front of the girls with his arms splayed out. He faced the camera and the oncoming danger—*protecting* "his" girls. Later, Gracie said she bet he thought it was Maddy who screamed, "Daddy!" It was what he made her call him. He must have known she knew he planned to kill her. But psychopaths have no empathy. Their fantasies have nothing to do with anyone but themselves.

I tackled Peewee to get to my Gracie, and I might have sort of trampled him on the way. But before that, as I passed the camera, I squeezed the little bulb thingy hanging down. We ended up with a fine photo of Peewee Libitski looking very surprised, and his captive maidens glad to see an enraged father and cop.

For a while, once I freed Gracie, I couldn't do anything but hug and rock her. A lot of snuffling and crying went on, and I won't say none of it was mine. Nobody hassled us until I was ready to work and Gracie said she needed her clothes and was starving. In the meantime, the team arrived and then the Crime Scene unit, along with Gladys and a social worker to help Maddy get past the first shock and dress and get cleaned up. Then they'd take her to her family.

As we were leaving, Maddy, who was clearly traumatized and moving slowly, said, "Wait. I want to speak to Jinx."

"Will you talk to Maddy before we leave?" I asked Gracie. "It's up to you."

"Of course!" she said. "I want to!"

"Hi, Jinx. You're okay?"

"My name is Gracie," Gracie said. "I'm fine. I'm glad *you're* okay."

"I wanted to thank you," Maddy said. "Not just for saving me. For stopping him. I used to be a fighter. I helped scared people stand up for themselves, the way you did for me. He took that away from me. But I won't always be like this. Can we get together when I'm myself again?"

Grace hugged her fiercely.

"Of course we can! I'd love it."

Later, I told Gracie an experience like that was never easy to get past. It left a lot of disturbing feelings behind, even if the traumatized person wasn't fully aware of them for some time.

"You mean that Maddy might never be the way she was before? When she said, 'When I'm myself again'?"

"No, she might not. But I was talking about you," I said.

I'm not sure she believed me.

* * * *

Gracie keeps telling her dad she knows all about PTSD. She doesn't think she'll have it. "We got the better of Peewee in the end," she keeps saying, "didn't we?" She keeps trying to remember everything for when she appears in court. Too bad the wire she was wearing conked out. But it did. Without a verbatim transcript, they'll really need her testimony. In school, in something called college application prep, when they ask what she thinks her strongest characteristic is, Gracie says, "Resilience."

* * * *

I hated having to take Gracie back to the station with me that day. She should have been at home, tucked into bed with a mug of hot chocolate and her old teddy bear. But there was no one at home to stay with her, and I was still on duty. Besides, I couldn't bear to let her out of my sight.

It didn't quite work out like that. She waited in the hall while I did a lot of paperwork. Then I took Peewee to booking. We were cuffed together because it was my collar. We marched right past Gracie. I wished she didn't have to see him again. I didn't much like her seeing me in that position either.

"Hey, kid," Peewee said, twisting to see her, his wrist straining against the cuff. "Was it all lies? Or do you really wanna be a writer?"

"I just said that, asshole," Gracie said.

"Language, Gracie."

She danced away from us, and I couldn't do a thing about it, what with the cuff locked around my wrist. It was some consolation that Peewee wasn't going anywhere either, except inside for a long, long time.

Gracie stuck her tongue out at my prisoner.

"I'm going to be a vice cop like my dad."

Elizabeth Zelvin's short stories appear in *Ellery Queen's Mystery Magazine* and *Alfred Hitchcock's Mystery Magazine* as well as *Black Cat* and will appear in *Jewish Noir II* in 2022. Liz writes the Bruce Kohler Mysteries and the Mendoza Family Saga. She has been nominated three times each for the Derringer and Agatha Awards. "A Breach of Trust" was listed in *Best American Mystery Stories 2014*. Liz edited the anthologies *Me Too Short Stories* and *Where Crime Never Sleeps*.

THE REMARKABLE CASEBOOK OF INSPECTOR GEORGE M. TREVELYAN (RET.)

THE WHITE CALF AND THE WIND

being a true account of the foiling of nefarious and malicious deeds in the village of Winslow, Dorset, in the winter of 1890.

MIKE ADAMSON

The winter of 1889–1890 was remarkably snow-free, but oh, the gales... The winds raged in off the Atlantic, or at other times blew from Scandinavia, and the scouring blast drove rain that seemed to penetrate the stoutest clothing like needles. I had settled in at the still-renovating Winterbourne Priory, on Chaldon Down, just west of my natal village of Winslow, on the Dorsetshire coast, and was passing my first winter there following my forced retirement from Scotland Yard. My right knee ached softly in the cold; the repairs were the best surgery could offer and I was no longer bitter that the Whitechapel riots of '88 had turned me from Detective Inspector to country gentleman, writing his memoirs. It transpired it was a life that had its moments.

Winslow was a small place a way back from the Dorset cliffs, and beyond the village bobby it relied for its policing on the constabulary of Weymouth, ten miles distant—and of course myself, retired as I was. PC Tommy McGovern was a good copper but when it came to anything more complicated than breaking up affrays amongst farm hands on a Saturday night or solving the theft of the odd chicken, all eyes had begun to swivel to me—despite the fact working detectives did not always appreciate the input of retired colleagues.

There had been a murder. Naturally, in the raw January weather, the day barely begun, I found Tommy knocking desperately at the stout old door of the priory, his broad face wind-chapped, sandy moustache damp and forlorn, and I accompanied him at once, with a seaman's oilskins and rubber boots over my warmest fare. We squinted into the wind that drove grey curtains of drizzle in from the English Channel as his pony trap rattled the muddy track to Seaview Farm on the dales above the village, and we spent a large part of the day taking statements, unravelling the relevant from the not. I made a detailed inspection of both the body and area before ordering nothing touched until an official party could arrive. The weather was chill, she would keep where she lay... I had seen a fair few bodies in my time, from the remainders of bar brawls to floaters in the Thames, and much worse, but Tommy was quite shaken. He would have driven me home, but the short winter day was wearing swiftly to a stormy dusk and he must get a telegram away to Weymouth, requesting their assistance first thing in the morning, then he needed to be home to his wife and a warm fire. I had him drop me at the King George in the highstreet, assuring him I would get my report ready for the Weymouth force, and take a room for the night.

The publican, Sam Jevvons, was the closest thing to a friend I'd made in the six months I'd been home in Winslow. His round countenance and silver hair welcomed me with a smile, his cheery wave, as I passed the double entryway, shutting out the gale with its hint of sleet. I hung my oilskin in the hall, fought out of my boots and stood them against a wall with other patrons' dripping footwear, then wiped my walking stick of the mud it had accumulated. A framed mirror dominated the entrance, and I took in my own bedraggled appearance, craggy clean-shaven features below dark hair overdue for a trim, droplets on the collar of my tweed jacket. My notebook and statements were safe in an inside pocket, and at this point I wanted only the hospitality of the house. Hot steak and kidney pie with mash and veg, and a tall stout to go with it—the pub had laid on hot fare as they had a crowd. Sam confided with an apologetic quirk of his bushy brows the best he could offer me for the night was an armchair by the fire, as all the rooms upstairs were taken. Half the village seemed to be here for the warmth and cheer, but there were travellers too, stranded by the storm, arriving in ones and twos during the day and deciding to let the gale blow itself out before they braved the country track to the next village.

I took little notice of the strangers as I busied myself with my meal, glad of the warmth of the old, timber-panelled pub with its heavy overhead beams, hanging horse brasses and lead-light windows. The King George had stood since the days of George II, had seen a hundred and seventy years of ships go by on the changeable Channel, visible from the upstairs windows over the rooftops and bare trees of the season, and seemed as permanent as the world. Legend had it as haunted, though in all the times I had stayed I had never felt creeping cold, heard voices, nor seen anyone who did not belong. But as the evening drew in, night falling strangely early as the gale continued to batter the street and fresh rain rattled at the windows, an odd pattern of associations began to develop that had my detective's instincts pricking—uncomfortably so.

I was working on my notes, reviewing my scrawl and writing up the statement to hand to the men from Weymouth tomorrow, but the general jocularity of the evening was somewhat obtrusive. Old Lawrence the carpenter played his fiddle from time to time, stories were told as the ale flowed, and my eye was drawn to the odd figure. Amongst the walkers and riders on their way across the downs we had some standouts. A small, worried-faced young woman in dark green skirt and jacket kept to herself, sipping tea, her eyes down; a doctor on his district rounds; a tradesman in town to mend piping. Yet, first among them was a sharp-faced man of indeterminate age in threadbare scarf and tatty bowler, who spoke with an east-end Cockney twang that took me back to my days on the beat. He was telling tall tales of wagers won at country race meetings, making overtly music-hall advances, with many a comedic wink, to the ladies in the cosy alcove known as *the snug*, and a small party of farm hands gathered about him. He seemed a bit too sharp, to me. I had seen performers before and pegged him for a carnival hand, a jack-of-all-trades, permanently on the make.

I shook off my thoughts and returned to my notes. Alice Turner had been a milkmaid at Seaview Farm, on the rolling land above the village; the child of a widowed mother in Winslow, she had taken work and acquitted herself well enough. She lived-in, workers' quarters were in an old stone cottage across the barn yard from the farmhouse, and no one had heard anything amiss; but when Alice had failed to show for the morning milking, Farmer Giles's wife had gone knocking at the cottage and discovered Alice on the floor, cold as ice with the marks of hands upon her throat. A lad was sent through the rain and wind to fetch PC McGovern, who came for me, and we were there by nine a.m. Giles was distraught. He had never encountered murder before, and he confided they had had a calf born a few days before, long out of ideal season, and the little one was an albino—sure to be taken as a bad omen by the more superstitious. He feared he would lose his labourers, with a murder hard on top of an unnatural event. I smoothed him over, then Tommy and I went through the cottage, Mrs Giles advising us on a few items that had disappeared, a gold trinket case precious to the girl, a cross she usually wore, a few pounds in savings. Plain theft could be the motive, but murder was a brutal act normally out of proportion to petty larceny. The culprit had left no sign even my practiced eye could discern, save footprints—in mud upon the bare boards of the cottage, several distinct marks that showed a right man's boot with a heel cleft on the side.

From that point onward, all I had was paperwork, and sorted the statements into a casefile, to be headed by my own detailed report. I was well through drafting it when the merriment at the bar broke my concentration and I closed my notebook, set aside my pencil, and looked around with a jaundiced eye. The cockney fellow was at the bar and seemed to be entertaining the farm lads with some slight of hand, but when wagers were mentioned my ears pricked up. He had all the air of a travelling fairground performer, and the moment he plucked a hard-boiled egg from the basket on the counter and bet the hands around him he could balance it perfectly upright, I sighed and left my corner booth, to sidle over.

The eggs were free to drinkers, and a dish of salt stood by the basket. They may not have seen the trick before, but it was nothing new to me, and I watched silently as first one man, then another tried to balance it upright—quite impossible. Then wagers were taken, a pound in total, and the sharp took back the egg and performed a little distraction, rattling off rhyming slang to the amusement of the Dorset ear, with bright smiles and much meeting of eyes, all of which concealed the fact the egg passed through his left palm for a moment before he made a theatrical flourish and all went silent—his tough fingers delicately manipulated the egg on the bar, and after long, tense seconds drew away, leaving it standing upright on its broader end. Gasps of wonder went round and my eyes met Sam Jevvons's behind the bar. He knew it was a trick as surely as I, and his fists were on his hips as he sniffed discord, hoping *I* might be the one to act.

Heads shook and hands went to waistcoat pockets for coin, but before anyone could pay up, I reached in and snatched the egg, held it up for all to see, and my eyes met the sharp's. He knew he was undone but brazened it out. "As you can see, squire," he said with a genial smile, "an egg is just an egg."

I held his gaze a long moment, then turned the egg to the hand next to me. "Lick it," I said softly, and when he hesitantly did so, he made a face. "Salty, isn't it?" My eyes went back to the sharp. "You moisten the egg, however you can, drop of beer on the bar, say. The salt is in your left palm. It sticks, creates roughness, and the egg balances on that." I returned the egg. "It's a trick, gentlemen." Then, to the sharp, "and if you happen to have three shells and a dried pea in your pocket, I suggest you leave them there."

Grumbles and stares went through the group in the sudden quiet and I sensed there may be measures as those so nearly cheated vented their spleen, but a rich voice in a well-to-do accent cut across the room, diverting all attention. "Bravo, sir! Well spotted. But these are straightened times, and one can hardly condemn a chap for raising the wherewithal of life with the skills to hand."

"What's wrong with a proper job?" somebody grumbled, but the patrons returned to their dominos, drinks, and chatter, and the moment passed. The speaker, a portly gent in decent city attire, grey hair trimmed close about a balding pate, watch chain stretched across his middle, rose and offered his hand.

"Allow me to present myself, sir. Professor Gerald McMurtry, late of Scottsdene Academy, Humberside." He spoke with gravity, his words very precise, very grand. "Fellow of the Royal Society, student of all matters philosophic, alchemic and metaphysical."

I hesitated a moment before taking the somewhat pudgy hand; something was oily about the man as he steered me away from the bar and into a vacant seat by a low table closer the hearth. "George Trevelyan," I replied. "Country gent, interested in all things…philosophical."

"Splendid," McMurtry beamed as he hove into his seat, and gestured to Sam. "Landlord, whatever this gentleman is drinking, on my account."

I half turned. "Cup of tea, thanks, Sam."

The professor chuckled as he took up his wine. "Really, sir, have you taken the pledge?"

"Not at all." My reply told him little. "What brings a distinguished fellow such as yourself to a flyspeck like Winslow, at such a time of year?"

The broad, somewhat florid face set in an expression of circumspection. "Professional, sir. I'm breaking my journey from Weymouth to Wooldridge Keynes—another 'flyspeck,' as you put it, but with rich research for a student of the strange."

"The strange?" I asked softly.

"The paranormal, sir. A ghost has been seen there far too often and a man of science has been requested to investigate."

"To...debunk it, you mean?" My question was met with sudden silence in the bar and I caught Sam's eye as he set down my tea before me. The air seemed brittle.

"Scepticism's a healthy thing, right enough," Sam murmured, "but this here pub has its non-paying resident too, you know. We'll not be offendin' Mistress Annie." He nodded to the portrait that hung in the snug, its gilt frame greened with age. The quaint, demure image of a woman in ornate jacket and bonnet dated from the time of the wars against Napoleon. "We do her honour, that she graces us with her favour."

"My dear sir," McMurtry began with a beaming smile, "perhaps I should room here once more on my return, for I would love to pen an account of your patron spirit." His eyes, almost laughing in their merriment, returned to me. "Debunk? Why no, sir! I'm an investigator who seeks the facts, and one does not do so with a closed mind." He sipped wine. "I agree unreservedly that the vaster majority of all such incidents have utterly mundane explanations, and many of them are indeed due to deception with intent to defraud. I have been associated with the Police on more than one investigation in other counties. From these labours has emerged the intriguing fact that when all such tommyrot and malice have been dispensed with, there inevitably remains a kernel of events which cannot be explained without resort to unreasonable levels of scepticism. That, sir, has become the consuming passion of my later years—the pursuit of *those* cases."

He had the attention of the whole bar. Eyes may not be on him, but all ears were flapping, and I chose my words with care. "Then you seek substantiation of occult claims?" Something in my tone communicated—to encourage him was in fact my intent. I had seen and done enough in my time, and omitted enough from my case dramatisations for *The Grosvenor Magazine for Gentlemen*, to have reserved my personal feelings upon matters too easily dismissed in an age of materialism. I was a realist, but that did not blinker me from looking beyond the limitations of the known. It also did not interfere with my ability to tell a charlatan at a hundred paces.

McMurtry finished his wine and set the glass down solemnly. "I make no claims to definitive knowledge, merely to an ongoing study which assembles information which may someday contribute to a coherent theory of the paranormal. A thoroughly scientific approach, grounded in reason, the observable, the measurable, to shed light upon the phenomena so entrenched in our folklore and society." His words were careful, and I felt myself challenged. My friends and neighbours cherished the belief a spirit walked this very building, and I had no wish to alienate them, yet how was I to maintain my credibility with the materialism so crucial to my vocation as a detective?

I sighed, sipped my tea and was aware the whole room was listening. "You are not alone in pursuit of such matters, sir," I admitted. "The whole field of spiritualism is gaining momentum, there is a veritable groundswell of interest all over the world. But when names like *Golden Dawn* and *Theosophy* are mentioned in the same breath, one is obliged toward caution."

Now he knew he fenced with someone at least fairly well informed. I threw out the comment and watched for him to spark. I had exposed the trick at the bar easily enough, but this scholar was a different order of ego. Even if he was absolutely sincere in his statements, he assumed the privilege of class, sat there like a lord in his hall—would he perceive bate and rise to it? Was I bating him because I was bored? Or was a copper's sixth sense at work?

"What proof would you have?" he murmured. "Would you...commune with spirits?" He took up a black bag at his side—a leather valise much like that carried by a doctor—and wrapped it in his arms somewhat protectively. The gesture seemed innocent enough, his eyes never leaving mine, and he folded his hands upon the bag. "Treasured papers, sir, the doings of my trade. It comforts me to keep them close."

I held his glance for long moments, then decided I had nothing to lose and everything to gain by calling his bluff. "Very well, Professor. Let's commune with spirits. How about the one said to walk these very halls?"

He smiled genially. "One cannot command spirits to appear. The odds of a particular wraith deigning to speak with mortals are astronomically against. Nevertheless, I will do my best."

"I'd like to see it," the cockney who still sulked by the end of the bar murmured. He wiped his lips with the back of a hard hand. "I've heard enough stories in my time."

"Yeah," was the first whisper from the green-skirted young woman with the mousy frown, her accent also London. "Come on, guv'ner, let's see it."

He looked around the expectant faces, the atmosphere suddenly pent. "Landlord, it's too bright in here. May we have the lamps turned down low?"

Sam made his way around the chamber, reducing each oil lamp to half strength, and when the fire was the brightest illumination McMurtry composed himself. "Absolute quiet, please, ladies and gentlemen," he murmured. "It takes intense concentration to reach for the spirit realm."

I had observed séances more than once when the Detective Branch was after confidence tricksters attempting to separate well-to-do elderly women from their cash with the voices of lost husbands. They operated to a pattern, were highly theatrical, and I had searched meeting rooms in advance looking for devices used to create illusion—sound, light, movement, whether mechanisms or hidden accomplices. They were even known to use ventriloquists to provide the voice of the dead. As nearly as I could tell, McMurtry was without any such aids and was not centralising the gathering's attention with a formal circle. Could he be on the level? I was aware of a certain misgiving—if he was entirely genuine, he may damage my cynicism, upon which a detective depended. If he was not, I may alienate my neighbours by demonstrating it. Perhaps I would be best served to observe quietly and applaud, whatever transpired.

McMurtry closed his eyes and breathed deeply, softly, expression entirely neutral. Firelight flickered on his jowly features and the only sound was the wind worrying the thatch and the intermittent beat of rain at the lead-lights. After a time, he stirred a little, seemed ill at ease, and his expression twisted, lips compressed. He began to murmur, incoherently at first, but then words became clearer.

"No rest, no rest... None for the wicked. And all's wicked as were never found out." His accent had changed, it sounded south-country, and his timbre was almost falsetto, as if a woman, or child, spoke. Glances went around and people stirred uneasily. "Three bags full... One for the master, one for the dame..." The nursery rhyme trailed off into nonsense, and he panted softly. Silence for a while... Then, eyes closed, his head rose, and he seemed to look around imperiously. "Who are you people?" was the stern question, his voice now a mellow baritone, the accent upper crust but without his native obsequiousness. "What are you doing here? Did I send for you? How dare you?! You'll get nothing from me, I should send for my footman and have you whipped to the door!" He panted, seemed distressed for a few moments, then lapsed into silence, chin on his breast and breathing roughly.

So far, I had seen nothing that could not be accomplished by any actor worth his salt, and I remained silent, watching the other patrons as much as McMurtry. With all eyes upon him, a pickpocket would be making merry and I was frustrated my back was to the fairground sharp. The formerly quiet woman was out of her seat, kneeling by the low table, her eyes shining as she stared at the professor, gracing others with her open, guileless smile.

Abruptly he began again, his tone gruff, wandering through qualities and accents. "Cold nights, cold days... Dunno yer born, you people. Coddled, the lot o' you! Lick o' Navy discipline's what you need, you'd see the world anew, an' that's a fact!" He panted, seemed to switch personality yet again, a bewildered quality appearing. "Is my Robert here? I've a message for my Robert. Where's Robert?" He gestured loosely across the bar. "There's a black dog sitting by your feet, there. He looks so happy..." More panting, then a hand was extended as if seeking something. "A token... A token. Something. Anything..."

I glanced around, people were unsure what was expected of them, but after a moment the mousy woman unclipped a crucifix from her throat and gently lay the gold piece in the professor's outstretched hand. She drew back, her eyes filled with wonder, and all waited expectantly.

"Kindness," he whispered, "so rare today..." He turned the cross in his fingers, eyes still blind to the world, and brought his hands together, the gold glinting in the firelight. And he began a muttering chant, words repeating though impossible to make out clearly. They rose to a gruff crescendo and his hands shook like an ague was upon him, until they drew apart, and all gasped, for the cross floated in space between them.

I sat forward, stared, blinked, made myself look harder, but there was no mistaking it. The cross was levitated between his palms, turning this way and that with trembling agitation, as if drawn by forces unknown. I had seen many a conjuring trick, but knew there were neither wires nor mirrors here, and my mind raced. *How* was he doing it? And a thrill of unease went through me to my core—not that it might be a supernatural event, but that, if I could not figure it out, there would be enough egg on my face to discredit me as a detective ever after.

Assumption 1—this was not what it appeared to be.

Assumption 2—the solution was staring me in the face if I could but recognise it.

The voice went on, strident now, commanding attention. "Truth will become manifest. Remember my words! As surely as day follows night, the Lord will frown upon this abandoned hamlet. Death shall follow in the train of ill-omen, as the snow-white calf heralds the shadows. Hear me! Hear me, and despair!"

I'm unsure who was the more surprised, him, me or the other patrons, when I leaned forward and snatched the cross from mid air with one hand and the bag with the other, rose in a whirl and limped a few steps to the bar, Sam Jevvons at my side. Gasps went around and the mousy woman knotted hands in her curls as if about to scream, while the sharp was off his stool with a face like a black cloud. McMurtry was still deep in his performance, pretending to regain consciousness with protestations of headache.

"Light," I grunted, and the serving lad made a circuit to turn up the wicks. When we had a golden glow to see by, I panted shallowly and looked at the cross. I knew how it was done—I *thought* I knew, and it was too late to turn back. To Sam I added, "do you have your pen knife, Sam?" He took it from a pocket and opened it, and before every eye I tapped the cross to it—which grabbed and clung tenaciously.

Eyes widened and McMurtry's look was like poison. In truth my own heart was racing like a stamping engine, for the consequences of being wrong did not bear thinking about, I'd be a laughingstock in the town of my birth. But the cross stuck and I breathed easier. I opened the bag, drew out a contraption of six horseshoe magnets in a frame that directed their fields upward, and shook my head. "*Dissimilar charges attract. Like-charges repel.* The cross is gold electroplated over magnetised steel. Well-understood physics, professor. You brought music-hall magic to the hayseeds, looking for the gullible, this gent from the East End is your supporting act—you covered for him when I exposed his trick—while the lady who handed you this is your audience-plant. Scientist? You're a confidence charlatan!"

My accusation hung a split second, then the cockney chap launched himself across the room with a snarl of rage, aiming to grab away the bag, and a short, black club had appeared in his hand as if from nowhere. He swung viciously, I wove back against the bar top and he tackled me down, landed a desperate left that split my cheek, then Sam's beefy fists were on him, dragging him wide. I shot out a hand to where my stick leaned against the corner booth and lashed out, took him in the knee and sent him sprawling.

And as he lost a few moments, stunned, I saw the broken heel of his right boot, and, at my side, the other contents of the professor's bag spilled upon the boards: amongst the bits and pieces gleamed a gold trinket box, a cross on a length of gold chain, a few sovereigns... The woman screamed now, and the professor was half out of his seat, hand going into his voluminous jacket as if, just perhaps, for a gun, and a moment later the publican's voice boomed out, freezing every soul, as he extended the ugly snout of a double-barrel shotgun, which I never had any idea he kept under the bar.

"That's far enough! The three of you, over by the fire, sit down and shut up! I'll have no affrays in my pub!" He jerked his head to his serving lad. "Billy, go fetch Tommy McGovern, we've need of him!"

I dragged myself off the floor and propped on my cane. "It's two birds with one stone, Sam. I couldn't be sure until he mentioned a white calf. One was born at Seaview Farm a few days ago. Giles hasn't mentioned it to a soul, so the only one who might possibly know such privileged local knowledge is whoever strangled Alice Turner this morning... And who has a broken heel to his boot."

Gasps went through the patrons who clustered back from the line of Sam's weapon, and the three tricksters kept their eyes down, knowing they would be under guard all too soon. The sharp was trembling visibly; what could have prompted him to murder the girl in the process of robbing her might come out in questioning, but made no difference to his fate, nor to that of his accomplices who had profited thereby. Heavens knew how many they had duped in the past as they wandered from county to county with their act.

I alone knew by how fine a margin I had plucked a solution from chaos and had cause to caution myself. I was far from infallible and this could have gone much more wrong than a bloody face. I was offered a bar towel and pressed it to my cheek as I looked around in the glow of the lamps, and saw faces reflected in the black of night at the windows. One seemed to appreciate my work, however, and I smiled back at the kindly female face, framed in an old-fashioned bonnet, who made full eye contact with me via the reflection, and nodded with an expression of satisfaction in my resolution of this supernatural fraud.

Until I realised no such person had been standing in the bar and glanced the other way in search of her—found no one, and looked back at the window, where the reflection had now vanished.

A cold hand brushed my spine and my heart fluttered, for against all cynicism, all materiality, I knew that face.

It looked serenely from the painting in the snug, revered by all as the spirit who watches forever over the King George hotel.

✗

Mike Adamson holds a Doctoral degree in Archaeology from Flinders University of South Australia, where he began teaching in 2006. Mike is a passionate photographer, a master-level hobbyist, and a journalist for international magazines. Nominated for several awards, Mike has placed more than 160 stories to date, totalling more than 750, 000 words in print. Catch up with his writing at "The View from the Keyboard," http://mike-adamson.blogspot.com.

ANNIE
ANITA MURPHY

The yellow house with the slanted roof is mine. It was my mother's house. It still holds all her precious things. Except for me, of course. She didn't find much precious about me. The cottage is a gift to me from my sister Mary. Her inheritance. She carries the guilt of being the good child, the one worthy of it all.

I slouch in the green velvet chair and watch the black squirrels chase one another up through the great elms. I haven't taken the train anywhere in ten years. "Take the early train Annie," Mary said. "Then Father Conklin can ride back with you."

Bloody Hell! What do I need the priest for, more penance?

Didn't Ma make sure I did enough before she died? She knelt in the box for weeks confessing my sins, or her version of them. Christ, what a time that was, her on her death bed spewing the evils of her daughter.

I asked her once if she confessed her own sin as thoroughly as she did mine? This resulted in a tirade of self-praise and more condemnation, the wayward daughter.

I kept her secret of the night Daddy died.

It was Mary who took me upstairs and stood me in the tub. I watched the water turn red and swirl down the drain and she scrubbed my skin more rigorously than she usually did. Mary was three years older than me. She never cried, at least not in front of me. She was always trying to make up for it all. Mary would defend me every time Ma went into one of her spiels about the fantasies of young children.

"What's a six-year-old know anyway?" She would say. "They're always making things up. Why that Annie was the worst child for telling stories."

He had come home from the pub full of whiskey, again. There wasn't another sound in the house but his voice in the kitchen, low and angry. That's how I know terror, my own heart beating deafens me. I crawled under the corner of the kitchen table. His hand was between her legs and he was clawing at her clothes. She pushed him hard and he staggered backwards, his head hitting the corner of the kitchen cupboard. Blood ran slowly across the slanted floor towards me. A river forming around my knees. I could see his eyes beneath the table, cold and starring. Cold like marbles. Ma screamed for Mary to get the doctor. Later she would say, "He just stumbled backward and fell."

I hear myself sigh heavily and glance at the clock. It's time to get ready. I have laid out my clothes. I decide on my black cashmere sweater tucked beneath the tailored camel skirt. I always loved the wide cherry-red patent-leather belt that went with it, cinched tight around my waist like a great butterfly. I'll wear a pair of Ma's silk stockings.

I climb the narrow stairs and run half the bath. A habit I have acquired over the years. I've grown impatient it seems. I glance in the mirror before I slide in. I'm pleased about looking forty-five when actually I teeter on the edge of a darker abyss. You know, that place where thousands of old ladies with saggy stockings disappear. It's a faceless place of freedom. At least for some.

I wait for the rest of the water to fill up around me, close the tap and listen for the familiar bang somewhere deep down in the bowels of the plumbing.

I haven't used fragrance on my skin since my last date. I try to recall that evening and cringe at my inability to remember his name. My half-submerged calves glisten with oil, shapely down to my narrow ankles. The curves will still dress up those black leather pumps quite nicely. I pull the saturated sponge over the length of my body, stopping to squeeze out a rush of the warm water over my breasts. I stretch out, close my eyes and pull the orange blossom fragrance deep into my nose.

I wonder what ugly stories my family has told. Probably the depression and all the rest of it. Family! Mary, she's got those six kids all grown up now. I don't know too much about them as adults. The oldest one Kathleen, I remember. She was a little spitfire with dancing blue eyes. She could drink any man under the table at fourteen, I worried she would end up like me but Mary made sure that didn't happen. Poor little thing, I can only imagine the amount of time she spent in the confession box.

I see out the window that a little mist has gathered above the stony shore. I love the mist. It means you don't have to look too deeply at what's beyond. The trip around the lake will be lovely this time of year.

I climb out and stand in front of the mirror looking at the length of my body.

"You don't have anything to be ashamed of, Annie Kelly."

The silk slip drops over my head and folds of coolness lightly touch my skin. It had been my mother's, nothing but the finest. She'd made it herself, white silk thread; the tiny forget-me-nots stitched delicately over the lacy top. I could have worn it with nothing over it, and I probably had sometime in the intervening years. My mother and her elegance: a picture of sobriety presenting the image of a perfect family. I had ruined it for her, she said, and she died hating me for that.

I pull the lower drawer in the dresser open and look at the packaged pairs of Beaver silk stockings. My mother had collected them before the war. "The war ended that," she said. "Like it did everything else. Silk went to make parachutes and ammunition sacks for the cause."

Carefully I select the pair with the seam down the back. I roll them onto my hand and gently slide them over my toes and up my calves. Jesus, I forgot how sexy they could make a woman feel. I clip them to the garter belt. There would be dancing tonight. It has been years since I danced. I look in the scrolled mirror of the dressing table. My large blue eyes sparkle and still no wrinkles to speak of. It shocks me at times, what I see in my own reflection. It catches me off guard.

The quick turn of my head, the flash of an image of thick black hair and eyes so blue and clear. It's such a lie, the clarity I mean.

There is just the lipstick left; it always determines the final performance. My heart races. I can't remember which shade of red I prefer. The tubes roll one against the other across the top of the dressing table, each fully extended. It's the dark red that makes my lips look full. I choose it and notice how perfectly worn it has been shaped by use and how it still slides with the same ease of a decade ago. Twisting it back into its cool gold case I press my lips one over the other.

I stand and give myself a final look of approval. I notice the red lipstick gives a harder look to my mouth than it did ten years ago. I shrug it off and wrap my shoulders in the grey woolen shawl before stepping out to the waiting cab.

The cab driver is a local man, married to Beatrice Jones, a woman I went to school with. Beatrice never had much of a life and I don't suppose Johnny made it any better. He opens the door for me, a cigarette hanging out of the corner of his mouth. His eyes look up every inch of my leg to see what he can see. "You're cutting a fine figure, Annie," he says as he climbs into the driver's seat. "Where you off to? Do you have a date Annie? Come on Annie, fess up," he says with his handsome grin.

"Never you mind where I'm going Johnny, and put that cigarette out, I don't want to smell," I say harshly.

"Awe come on now Annie, you might find it nice to smell like me," he says. Johnny has charm that turns every woman's head and not a cruel bone in his body.

"You're married, Johnny, and besides I'm not going out with anyone, I'm going to visit Mary for a couple of days. One of the young ones is getting married." That settles him for a while and we chat idly about Mary and the family.

"Give Mary my best, Annie and I hope you have yourself a whale of a good time. You deserve that Annie Kelly, you've kept yourself locked up in that house far too long." Funny how he made it sound like self-punishment.

We pull into the station. Johnny holds the door and I hesitate a bit before stepping out. Smiling, I give him the fare and he tips his hat, looking just plain gorgeous.

I look more like the successful businesswoman I used to be than an aunt going to a wedding. I'm out of date, I suppose, but not so terrible. I always bought good clothes. Quality always transcends time. Ma used to think it such a waste. And indeed, dropping out of the work world quickly left me in poverty after the savings were gone. They once called me brilliant, I sold my soul for that. I was an oddity, a woman in business. It was hard to keep a job if you were married, pregnancy got you fired. I chose the work ahead of the hell my mother lived. A choice that brought its own darkness at the hands of men. Birth control was illegal. I don't know what kept me from getting pregnant, whether it was just luck or maybe I was just barren. Who knows?

I slide into a blue-grey upholstered seat of the empty rail car, marveling at how comfortable it is compared to the old ones. I rode the train every day back then and my mother waited for my arrival each night. I had started out as her shining star, soon to become her greatest disappointment.

"You're weak!" she raged. "Just like your father."

There was some truth to it. The whiskey brought many working days to a celebratory close. We'd drink to our successes down at the pubs. Usually I'd stagger off to the nearest motel with one of my colleagues.

It's been a long time since I felt a man. I wonder at times what it would be like to renew the feeling. It only crosses my mind once in a while when late at night I slide my hand inside my underwear. It's odd how the memory of it fades.

The train pulls out, cruises for a few minutes, then stops at the next station. An older man, slight with greying hair, and wearing a perfectly fitted suit takes a seat across the aisle from me. Suddenly I turn from his appraising eyes with a sense of panic. There is something familiar about him.

"Excuse me," he says. "You look familiar, do you work in the city?"

I smile and say, "Not anymore, I've been retired for a few years."

"Where did you work?"

"Oh, I am sure you wouldn't know, it was a long time ago."

Why and how have I agreed to this conversation? Why did I agree to take this trip at all? I suddenly know I have to go back home. The train pulls into the next station and I rush to the exit and down the platform. I cross over to wait along the track for the return train home. I tell myself Mary will understand if I say I have come down with the flu.

I hear footsteps on the concrete and I turn to see the man from the train coming behind me. I think that he must work somewhere close by. No. That can't be. He's crossed over with me to get the train back. Shaken I move quickly and look back to see him almost within arm's reach. I stop and step sideways to let him by. He stops. I am pressed against the cold cement and my heart is pounding in the side of my head. My fingers press against the wall.

"I know you," he says. "I know we have met before."

"No, I don't know who you are, now leave me alone!" My eyes dart up and down the platform grasping for anyone but there is no one. His face hovers just inches from mine with cold blue eyes. Terrified, I lower mine to that place just above his grey striped tie. My mind races, looking for an escape.

He tilts his head back, grabs my arm and pushes me harder to the wall. "We will see." He pauses as he moves himself up against me, "Now won't we? You see few people take this train anymore. We can have a little time, can't we? I know what you like. I've had you before." He pushes against me, his hand creeps up my thigh, his mouth pushes on my lips. I go with it, searching for a way out. His French cologne is suffocating. Nausea sits in my throat.

My rage overflows, all those years of just going with it. He feels me give in, his fingers dig for the edge of my underwear. I place my hands on his chest. I let them linger a bit then shove him hard and he staggers backward. He looks at me for just a moment with terrified eyes.

Then he's gone. I hadn't heard the train. I don't hear it now. I see it, window upon window flashing by. I climb up the stairs and cross back over. My train is still waiting to take me to Mary's.

I get back on.

The attendant enters the car and I look out the window. "It's a misty morning ma'am, I hope you're enjoying the trip."

I smile and nod, "I love the mist."

Anita Murphy is a Canadian suspense writer. She is prolific and writes in many genres, is an active participant in writers guilds and creative writing programs, and is the author of a published book of poetry, *The Red Horse*. Anita's work embraces the short story and her other creative profession, art. She is currently completing a degree in Creative Writing.

SANITY CLAUSE

MAX DEVOE TALLEY

Barry Shipman waited on the corner, slapping his gloved hands together and stamping his feet. The hood of the sweatshirt underneath his coat helped, but his nose went from numbness to feeling pain. Could you get frostbite of the nose? He'd seen photos of Mount Everest hikers who'd lost toes or fingers on their frozen treks, but couldn't remember any blackened noses.

He shivered as he stood on 27th Street and Park Avenue in Manhattan listening to the bell jingling in the distance. It served as a kind of clock or timer counting down the moments until he acted. The tinkling grounded him and reminded him why he had come.

Christmas season didn't strike Barry as the ideal time to murder someone. Though it was not a scenario he'd dwelt upon, having never killed anyone before. The Monday before Christmas retained happy memories for him. The spirit of goodwill, the sharing of niceties, and the promise of humanity putting aside their selfish pursuits for a moment—whether authentic or forced by a collective, commercial tidal wave. He felt those things too, but needed to make a moral exception this Christmas.

In a few days people would get manic with last-minute shopping. Not to mention the social tensions of pleasing family-members, of being thrown together with relatives loved and those despised. If Barry had been given a choice when to kill, he would have picked after the holidays, during that bleak trough of early January 2020, when the next year arrived newly born and barely sentient. A dark, depressing time.

Barry planned to skip town before then. Unless something went inconceivably wrong, he'd be rolling south toward palm trees by dawn. He hated winter in the tri-state area. Most years, the conditions became intolerable around New Years. This December, unfortunately, an Arctic air mass gripped the region by the family jewels early on and it had remained at record low temperatures ever since.

"Excuse me," said a pedestrian dodging around Barry's stationary form. "Merry fucking Christmas."

"Same to you," Barry replied. He heard the sidewalk Santa's jingling bell and again went over his plan, again imagined his escape to Florida. Last winter he traveled to Southern California, the year before to Phoenix, Arizona—but that hadn't proved warm enough.

* * * *

A week ago Barry was summoned from his miserable apartment off the New Jersey Turnpike to meet with Ron Marino at his Paramus office atop a pizza parlor. Just across the Hudson River from Manhattan but a world away. On the face of it, the request was no big deal. Ron served as an "associate." Not a made man, but a facilitator or helper for the big boys. He had suggested places for Barry to rob in the past and even recommended partners for two-man jobs. This time however, Ron had sent muscle in a car to make sure Barry accepted the invitation, and that perturbed him.

Barry tried to pry information from his driver-escort Phil, but the man's grayish slab of a face could have been carved from stone, and his communication skills ranged from grunts for *yes* and *no*, to the occasional, "let's go" or "come on" when spoken language became absolutely necessary. Barry was a wiry, nimble guy, perfectly suited to climb fire escapes or squeeze through narrow entry spaces. He avoided fighting other people—especially if they stood taller, weighed more, and carried weapons. So he shut-up when Phil told him to and stared in silence through the window of the brown Lincoln. They drove the eastern slice of Jersey that people warned of, that comedians joked about, as a sulfur gas odor mingled with the windblown garbage stench from the hundred-acre Kearny landfill.

In the upstairs office above Best Paramus Pizza, Ron got up from his desk grinning. "Barry, my man." When he embraced Barry, the smell of tomato sauce and nicotine, of cologne and musky BO washed over him. It was a complicated aroma that Barry had inhaled for much of his fifty years of life. That hug, followed by Ron waving Phil away, both relieved and relaxed Barry. If he had been in serious shit, there would have been no pleasantries. The suggestion of a meeting just a ruse for a final haunted ride to perdition.

"Sit." Ron gestured at a plush leather chair. After pouring them both a shot of Maker's Mark on the rocks, Ron sat back down and slumped forward, resting his elbows on the desk. "We've got a kind of situation, Barry, and we need help in resolving this thing." He palmed the sparse dark hair back on his scalp.

Barry knew who "we" referred to.

"You and I have always helped each other, so I know you'll want to do your part to make things right."

"Of course." Barry leaned in to show enthusiasm even if he only felt confusion. "Is there a job you need me on? I'm in. And you know I'd do it gratis since you got me plenty of scores in the past."

"Good, good." Ron cracked his knuckles. "Don't know if you heard about the robbery a month ago at a Fast Loans nearby in Passaic..."

"Uh, no, I didn't." Barry kept his eyes steady on Ron and allowed no facial twitches.

"Sloppy, amateurish job." Ron winced. "Not your style. The two dipshits involved were too stupid to realize it was a front, money laundering and such. They were stealing from my employers." He sighed while shaking his head. "Only took twenty large. Not a huge amount, but a major show of disrespect."

"Sure, I get it," Barry said. "A pair of dick-brains. Want me to ask around for their names?"

"No." Ron approached Barry's chair. "One of them was Sam Jacobs. Name ring a bell?"

"Sam?"

"Yeah, the guy you did a job with four years ago. Remember, before you pulled an eighteen month stretch in East Jersey State?"

"Oh, right, right. *That* Sam." Barry kept his expression rubbery and casual. "Any leads on his whereabouts?"

Ron's smile appeared created with great pain. "We found him. Unfortunately, my man Phil"—he pointed toward the door—"was over-enthusiastic and we lost Sam before extracting his partner's name." Ron perched on the edge of the desk. He stared at Barry, his brow scrunched in contemplation.

Thinking among criminal associates rarely led to good things so Barry interrupted the oppressive void of silence. "I'm happy to find the other dude."

"I'm ninety-nine percent certain it was his cousin, Justin. Another stupid prick who gets caught and locked-up every few years."

"I met Justin while I was doing time," Barry said. "Total dumb-fuck."

"Yeah." Ron rubbed at his lips with two fingers. "So I need you to eliminate him fast, like within the week."

The turn of events seemed both beneficial and troubling. "Ron, I want to help," Barry said, stuttering, "but I'm a porch climber, a second story man." He wiped at his damp forehead. "You know I'm not hired juice. I'm no good at that."

"Sure, sure." Ron again smiled without joy. "See, if I present two deceased schnooks to my employers, it ends there. If they investigate—and they will—they'll torture Justin and he'll give out names. People he worked with, guys in the slammer, people he wants to finger. Your name, since he knows you from prison and from your jobs with his cousin Sam..." Ron clipped a thin cigar but didn't light it. "If you don't handle this, we're all in trouble. Especially you."

Phil reentered the office with a black leather satchel and unzipped it. Inside lay a selection of knives, along with a hook and a pike.

"Your target is running scared after Sam got popped, but he's definitely been spotted in downtown Manhattan." Ron's voice became a whisper. "No guns. Too loud. Stab him or slit his throat. You know the deal. You offed a guy once, right?"

Barry nodded. He'd sliced someone's arm when they tried to rip off his wallet outside a Bronx bar, but then exaggerated the story into a brutal execution by stabbing to keep him safe in prison. So Barry could shower with impunity. "But, I..."

"Don't worry, we'll know Justin's exact location over the weekend. You'll go into Manhattan at night, do the job, and head out—far away."

"Well, I planned—"

"Don't tell me the destination." Ron pulled an envelope from a desk drawer. "Five hundred should get you pretty far. I'm not paying for the job itself because it's what you call life-preservation."

"Understood."

On the half-hour drive back home, Barry watched the marshy terrain around the Meadowlands Sports Center flash by. Phil, the silent driver, sped from I-80 onto 95, merging with the Jersey Turnpike near Secaucus. Along the foul Hackensack River, Barry saw black smoke gushing from factory chimneys, the flames rising atop gas towers above the Turnpike, and considered his dilemma. He really had no choice. Murder the only option. Today's meeting had been the first he'd heard of Sam's demise. He assumed the guy was hiding out somewhere. Sam Jacobs, *his* partner in the robbery of Fast Loans in Passaic. No wonder no one else had hit that joint before. A mob front. If Barry didn't take out Cousin Justin, his ass was cooked.

* * * *

On Friday, Barry met Debra at the bar inside Palisades Grill on the cliffs overlooking the twinkling sparkle of Manhattan and the colored lights of ships cruising up and down the Hudson River. He had flirted with her before, but those times she'd been married or seeing someone.

Debra lowered her long eyelashes in confession mode. "I'm recently single," she said in a hushed voice, as if admitting to a rare disease.

"That's no crime," Barry replied. He knew Debra was the type of person who couldn't survive alone for long, the type who preferred a bad relationship over waking up solitary in the world, having to face oneself, without direction, without appreciation. "So what are you doing for the holidays?"

"Drinking." She laughed. "I hate this time of year. My parents are both dead and I don't speak to my sisters in Pennsylvania."

"I'm going to Florida, next Tuesday or Wednesday."

"Really?"

"Yeah, I can't stand the cold and all the false Christmas cheer," he said. "I mean Christ, I'm fifty."

"But you could pass for late forties."

Barry didn't reply. Instead he studied his drink and surreptitiously ogled Debra's shapely figure, imagining her in a bathing suit stretched out on the beach. "Why don't you join me, spend a week down south? We could hit Miami or Palm Beach, then even the Florida Keys."

Debra's head hung loose from the alcohol but she twisted her neck to study him. "That sounds great, but I'm pretty broke and still getting over Ray-Ray."

"Ray-Ray?" Barry held an innate suspicion of people with two first names that were identical. "Listen, I'd be covering travel and lodging." He still had seven grand leftover from the Fast Loan job and the desire to spend that dirty cash fast.

Debra leaned close to him from her neighboring bar stool. "I need a vacation and warm weather, I really do." She gave him a cock-eyed glance. "Would we be sharing one room?"

"No, I could get you a separate room nearby. I'm not expecting—"

"How about a two-room suite?" she asked. "I don't plan things in advance. I like to decide my sleeping arrangements on the fly." She nestled her head of big Jersey hair on his shoulder. She whispered, "You're not bullshitting me?"

"Hell no." He felt as honest as someone with a criminal background could feel, and noticed the arousal when she brushed a hand up his leg.

"I'm not going home with you tonight but I will go to Florida, if you call me." Debra snorted. "I don't believe you'll call."

"Pack your sexiest bathing suits."

"Bikinis but no thongs." She wagged a finger. "Stopped wearing them after thirty."

"Same with me."

She gave Barry a few sloppy kisses, then staggered outside when her Uber ride pulled up. The bartender handed him napkins to wipe off the bright red lipstick smears. He couldn't explain why, but he felt an odd love for Debra. The sense of not really knowing someone so you could fill in the blanks, imagine them as exactly the person you needed.

* * * *

Standing on Twenty-Seventh Street of Manhattan in the frigid cold, Barry could no longer focus on Debra. A distraction. He'd meet her after midnight as planned. First he had to do his job, then get cleaned up at his hotel room, then haul ass to Penn Station for their Amtrak train ride to Florida. He'd been born in 1969, the same year his favorite New York movie with Jon Voight and Dustin Hoffman came out. Seeing it at age eighteen on VHS and again later on DVD, Barry realized he fit into that late sixties era. Poor hustlers and small-time-crooks eking out a living in the harsh landscape of a filthy and dangerous Times Square. He couldn't relate to the modern-day city where everything was expensive, shiny, and out of reach.

Over the last hour Barry circled the block several times attempting to hand out cards. New Yorkers moved in a hurry and walked even faster during icy weather. They were especially adept at sidestepping around a hooded stranger wearing ragged clothing and offering cards for a nonexistent massage parlor in Brooklyn. To add to his created character, he talked aloud: muttering, spitting, asking questions. Just as Barry's target stood nearby hiding in plain sight, he too was stalking in plain sight. If anyone described what went down to the police later, they would peg him as a mentally disturbed, homeless man.

New York was the city that never slept, but on the Monday night before Christmas, car and pedestrian traffic thinned out after ten. The bell-ringing from Santa became sparser, less spirited. The cue for Barry to make his move.

Ron had explained over the phone on Saturday. "Yeah, we tracked Justin down in Manhattan. He worked Times Square dressed as a Pirate of the Caribbean for tourist photos, then scored a job with the Salvation Army as a sidewalk Santa in the Grammercy Park vicinity. So you need to do the thing we spoke of—soon."

Barry had psyched himself into the act out of desperation. Life or death. *His*. Still, as he walked in a shuffling stagger from Park Avenue South toward the chiming bell, he decided to make sure this Santa wasn't some hapless fool in the wrong place at the wrong time.

Santa had retreated into an alcove formed by a descending stairway on one side and a jutting four-story brownstone on the other. The spot shielded him from the bracing evening wind and kept him—for the most part—out of sight, about thirty feet west of Lexington Avenue.

Since Barry circled the block numerous times in his disguise, Santa showed no apprehension when he approached. Not until he got up close.

"Hey, beat it," Santa said. "I've got no money for you. Done for the night. Step off."

Barry feigned moving three paces away and checked the street for a break in car traffic. When the cross-street lights turned red, he lunged at Santa, knocking him off balance against the iron gate of an alleyway that separated the two buildings.

"Justin?" Barry tore the bogus white beard off the startled man's face. "It is you."

"Fuck, Barry, is that you? I didn't expect you to be disguised."

Barry had no time for small talk, only action. He jabbed the blade into Justin's stomach but instead tore into the massive padding used to create Santa's girth. Before losing his nerve entirely, he brought the knife up and sliced at Justin's neck. A sharp scraping noise sounded. Justin wore a protective collar, as if expecting an attack. *What the hell?*

Justin kneed Barry in the groin and his knife went skittering across the pavement. The fist extruding from Justin's red Santa sleeve gripped another larger knife. "Thanks for making this easy." He slashed at Barry's side, tearing away layers of clothing.

Barry felt the cold air but no pain so he dodged away. "Making what easy?" He retreated as the knife whistled through the air, just missing his chest.

"You delivered yourself right to me." Justin smiled, his scarred face extra ugly under the sagging red cap and pom-pom.

"I delivered?"

"You don't steal twenty large from *them* and walk away."

Total realization struck. Barry had been set up—the target of this hit, not the hired juice. Hell, Ron was cackling back in his Paramus office, betting that they'd both take each other out.

An adrenaline rush of fear helped Barry grab Justin's right forearm and bend it back to the point of pain. He hammered it against the iron gate until the knife dropped. Before Justin could recover, Barry took the pike from his pocket and, using all his weight, pounded it into the guy's heart. Justin's eyes went wide with fear before glazing over. His hands flopped around as his fat Santa body trembled and shook until he collapsed to the sidewalk.

"Mommy, Daddy, that man just killed Santa Claus!" a young girl shrieked from the corner of Lexington Avenue.

Barry panicked. Unable to retrieve the impacted pike, he left it lodged in Justin's chest and hustled west toward Park Avenue.

"Somebody stop that guy," a man shouted.

Barry brushed by pedestrians, but glancing back noticed them taking photos, maybe even videos. *Fuck, fuck, got to make it to the subway*. His side ached like he was getting a stitch, but when he rubbed it, the flesh felt wet and warm. That asshole Justin *had* cut him. He just hadn't registered it in the bitter cold.

Barry heard a siren. It could be for anything or it could be for him. Park Avenue was just a half block away, then another block south to the subway entrance. People stood massed ahead of him, pointing and shouting. *How had this thing escalated so quickly?* He registered the street construction, a large hole in the asphalt surrounded by safety lights and fencing, and darted off the sidewalk toward it. Without thinking, he plunged down into a low tunnel running just below street level. In one direction, seeping hot steam clouded the passage, so he moved back east toward Lexington.

In about fifty yards he found a metal ladder leading downward. *Don't get caught, don't get caught*. He descended into a pitch black subway tunnel and waited until his eyes adjusted to see the faint shine of rails below. Water dripped from above and chunks of granite lay across sections of tracks. Barry knew the Lexington Avenue line yawed west below 42nd Street and subsequent stops were on Park Avenue. He must be on a leftover spur from the moribund Third Avenue or Second Avenue Line. Manhattan was spider-webbed with abandoned train tracks.

Flicking a lighter, he got his bearings and began moving north. Just six blocks to the Penn Station vicinity and he'd find an avenue of escape back to the surface. The dank tunnel smelled of entombed death. A chilling breeze came from somewhere ahead along with the phantom rumbling of distant invisible subways on other lines. Barry hurried along the tracks but sloshed through puddles. Coming out of a deep one he studied his unfamiliar-shaped boot. A large gray rat sat atop it gripping the sides. "Shit," he shouted and stamped his boot down on dry ground until the creature scampered away.

His vision adjusted further and he could discern other people—carrying on, living their lives. The urban legends were true. They groaned or laughed as he passed by them. Some smoked cigarettes at the edges of the tunnel where they'd built ramshackle shelters. Overhead, the faint sound of carolers on the street singing "Fa-la-la-la-la..." filtered down.

The tracks Barry followed veered left and crossed another set before dead-ending in a mess of broken rails and rubble. He sparked the lighter and decided to follow the neighboring tracks north. A grimy hand grabbed his elbow. "Stay here. Don't go." He shook loose, having no plans to join their subterranean civilization. Another three blocks and he was safe. Barry had never identified with Ratso Rizzo, the sickly loser, but with Joe Buck. He imagined arriving in Florida and changing into short-sleeved shirts, ditching his winter clothes like Jon Voight had.

He smiled wide, almost delirious, and picked up the pace, ignoring hissing voices saying, "Stop," and "Come back." God, he was tired but he needed to move faster. Outrun time. Once above ground he'd make his way to Hotel Metro on 35th Street, take a shower, put on fresh clothes, bandage his side and get to Penn Station by 12:30 to meet Debra. All the hard shit lay behind him: robbery, murder, a bleak Christmas. Barry ran and ran, picturing Debra sprawled across his Florida hotel bed tipsy and naked, her tan lines showing and the moist heaven waiting. Their love would blossom and grow under a wintry sun.

His head felt woozy, maybe he was catching a cold, but who cared? From somewhere he heard Harry Nilsson singing "Everybody's Talkin'," except the words had ceased and Nilsson was mouthing, "Waugh... Waugh-wah-wah-waugh." Just one more block. Barry could already hear Debra saying she loved him as he descended while she held him. And it was so goddamned cold in that tunnel, but in the midst of the smell of ash and soot and all the dust that a corpse eventually decays into he felt something good. The sun rose behind him, heat growing, as its light illuminated the darkness beyond. Barry laughed so hard that tears streamed down his face. *Florida, here I come*! And the sun got warmer and brighter on his back, the tunnel rattled and vibrated, so Barry let himself go. Total relaxation. He may have even pissed his pants like Ratso Rizzo did on the Greyhound bus, but it didn't matter. Nothing mattered.

He could hear the Greyhound's horn. *Merry fucking Christmas*. Shrieking noise, a shuddering vibration, and the light grew brighter, and Barry got to his destination in an instant.

Max Talley was born in New York and lives in Southern California. His writing has appeared in *Vol.1 Brooklyn, Atticus Review, Entropy, Fiction Southeast*, and *Litro*. He won the Best Fiction Contest at *Jerry Jazz Musician* magazine. Talley's novel, *Yesterday We Forget Tomorrow*, was published in 2014 and his crime thriller, *Santa Fe Psychosis*, is forthcoming from Dark Edge Press. He teaches writing at Santa Barbara Writers Conference and at Santa Fe Workshops.

THE BORSCHT BELT BURGLARY
MARLIN BRESSI

Charlie Slutsky had the Nevele Resort in Wawarsing, so it seemed only natural that his former childhood rival should open his own hotel in Loch Sheldrake, which he did, and christen it the Neetenin Lodge. Slutsky's hotel, as any veteran Borscht Belt vaudeville trouper will tell you, is "eleven" spelled backwards.

"I was torn between calling the joint Neve's Place or the Hotel Eno," Harry Katz had explained during my interview, "but it was my wife, Rina, who suggested the Neetenin Lodge. They once had a lot of Indians running around the Catskills, or so I've heard, and she thought the name sounded authentic. Say, Archie, what was that tribe called again?"

"Leni Lenape?" I ventured. Having been born and raised in Scranton, I wasn't overly familiar with the pre-Columbian history of the Catskills. All I knew was that the Neetenin Lodge, like all the large Borscht Belt resorts, desperately needed a house dick. Now that Grossinger's and Nevele had opened their doors to the *goyim*, there had been a maddening rash of burglaries, sprinkled with the occasional felonious battery. From what I had been able to ascertain from Rina Katz, I was the only one who had applied.

"Lenny Lend-a-Pie? I think I booked him once in aught-six," replied Harry. "Prop comic, right? He opened for Boris Thomashefsky, if I recall." I attempted to steer the conversation back to the house detective position. He asked if I happened to be Irish. I told him my surname, Newcomb, was English in origin.

"That's too bad," said Harry. "The Irish are really good at your line of work. Then again, the English are practically neighbors, so maybe you'd be good at it too. Hey, the Sheriff of Nottingham was English, wasn't he? You seem like a real mensch. Just don't go counting the till, all right? So, when can you start?" I was taken aback; Katz hadn't even asked about my credentials! I was prepared to tell him a lengthy story about my brief tenure as a Pinkerton agent or my time working security with the Braddigan Brothers circus, where I had rubbed elbows with my fair share of performers and ex-vaudevillians.

Before long, I discovered that Rina Katz hadn't been exaggerating about the thefts and break-ins; every week in the Catskills there was some criminal mystery that needed solving. In February, a burglar using an assumed name had checked into Kutscher's, a few miles down the road, and had ransacked a couple of bungalows, making off with a few furs and enough silk scarves and handkerchiefs to make Beau Brummell green with envy. Though the local constabulary caught the thief, the burglaries continued unabated. In March, I knew the Neetenin Lodge had fallen victim to the crime wave when Harry Katz stormed into my bungalow at three o'clock in the morning wearing nothing but a dressing gown. It was a frigid night in the Catskills. My powers of deduction, impaired by a night of dancing and one too many sangarees, led me to believe that his clothing had been pilfered.

"Gladly I would trade my coat and pants for what those *gonifs* stole from me!" he bellowed, and after rubbing the sleep from my eyes I followed him into the frosty night. In the lodge's office I found Rina on her knees, sobbing hysterically in front of the safe.

"We're ruined!" she gasped between her maelstrom of tears.

"The crook made off with our take," said Harry. "Not just tonight's take, Arch. Our entire week's take." I ran my fingers through my hair and, forgetting my place, demanded to know why daily deposits hadn't been made. Harry stopped shivering long enough to point out the window. "You see a bank out there? I'm looking for one, but all I see are trees. You want I should start depositing our take in the hole in that tree trunk? Or how about I bury it beneath that big yellow pine? Oh, I see a bank all right! It's called the First National Bank of Bupkes!"

"All right, I see your point," I sighed, joining Rina on the floor. A cursory examination of the safe left me stymied; there were no gouges or chisel marks to be seen. There wasn't a scratch on the thing—it looked as if it had just come from the factory. To my mind, this meant only one thing. "The thief must've known the combination," I said. "Obviously, this was an inside job."

"Our staff would never do such a thing," Rina protested. "Why, they're like family. *Mishpocheh*, they are! I say we're dealing with a master safe-cracker." The way Harry nodded indicated that mine was the minority opinion. But who was the detective? I told Harry that he might know a buck-and-wing from a shuffle-off-to-Buffalo, but in matters of criminal investigation, I was the expert. The bluff seemed to work. The biggest mystery I had ever solved was figuring out who had stolen thirty pounds of raw meat from the circus cat man's icebox. It turned out to be Hilda, the Bearded Chanteuse.

"But Archie, the only one who knows the combination to the safe is Rina," said Harry, I looked at Mrs. Katz and she gave an embarrassed nod.

"It's true, detective. Harry's never been much for numbers."

"You know something? That just might explain why we're in the black," mused Harry.

"In the red, dear," corrected Rina, swiping a wayward tendril of curly black hair from her forehead.

"See what I mean, Archie? Rina's the one with the business sense around here. A regular J.P. Vanderbilt she is," said Harry. I'd been at the Neetenin Lodge for two only months, but I felt as if I had taken a wrong turn and ended up in a vaudeville skit. I was expecting Harry and Rina to slather on some pancake makeup and break into a chorus of *Oh, By Jingo!* at any minute.

"So what are you going to do?" implored Rina. I told her that I would need to take a few notes, and Harry rolled up the top of his desk and produced a pencil and notepad. As the Katzes answered my questions, I jotted their responses onto the paper. The robbery must've taken place after eight thirty that evening, after the last patrons had arrived at the lodge. Payday wasn't for another two days—all the performers and lodge staff were paid at the end of the week—so there would've been no reason to open the safe until morning.

"I came to the office on a whim, Archie," explained Rina. "Did you ever wake up in the middle of the night with a strange feeling that something wasn't right?"

"Who was working tonight?" I asked. Harry gave me the names of a half dozen busboys, a handful of cooks, two maids, and the bartender.

"It couldn't have been Clancy, he didn't get a chance to leave the bar all night," said Rina, who had been flittering between the bar and kitchen all evening like a butterfly caught in a tempest. "We've been very short-staffed this week. Tonight I was the usher, hat-check girl, tummler, *and* dishwasher."

"Talk about a quick-change act!" said Harry.

"Naturally, the busboys and cooks couldn't have done it," Rina continued. "They each got a couple of five-minute breaks, but that wouldn't be long enough to crack a safe, stash the loot, and return to work, would it?"

"No, I reckon it wouldn't," I admitted. The office of the Neetenin Lodge was in a newly-constructed wing off the main building, down a long, narrow corridor, about as far from the kitchen and stage as the performer's bungalows. "Which leaves only the maids," I added. I asked the Katzes what they knew about the two girls, Judith and Laverne.

"Judy's my niece," said Harry. "Sweet kid. Lazy as a sloth, messy as a hobo, and just between you and me, her piano ain't always tuned to right pitch, if you catch my drift. But a sweet kid, nonetheless."

"And Vernie is engaged to Moshe Adler, the Broadway impresario," explained Rina. "She isn't exactly in danger of headlining the county poor farm. She just works here because she likes to watch the shows. She prefers vaudeville to legitimate theatre. She'll be moving to Brooklyn after the wedding."

"Hey, are you calling my joint illegitimate?" interrupted Harry with mock indignation. "I'll have you know, Mrs. Katz, that Neetenin's mother was a luxury hotel and her father was the ritziest boardinghouse in the Bowery."

I told the Katzes that I'd get started on the case first thing in the morning. As the owner and his wife made for the door I grabbed Rina by the sleeve.

"Wait," I said. "We better use the main entrance. The ground is damp and there's a good chance our thief went out through the office door. At sunrise I'll check for footprints." I took off my coat and handed it to Harry, who was still in his sleepwear. "And you, *bubelah*, put this on. The last thing we need is for you to catch pneumonia."

As we went to our respective bungalows, I heard Harry say to his wife: "What did I tell you, Rina? Is he a mensch or what?"

* * * *

The combination of crisp mountain air and coffee kept me awake, and as I waited for the morning sun to peek over the bruise-colored horizon and bathe Shawangunk Ridge in brilliant shades of magenta and ochre I attempted to shake from my brain the unsettling notion that Rina Katz was the culprit. She was the only person on the premises who knew the combination to the safe.

But why would she do such a thing? To teach her husband a lesson about fiscal responsibility? To appease a kleptomaniacal urge she had kept hidden for fifty-five years like the entrance to a pharaoh's tomb? I wondered if it could be some sort of crank, a joke perpetrated on the *goy* newcomer by a couple of old-time yuksters. Perhaps Harry and Rina manufactured the burglary because they wanted to see their new house dick in action. Could it be a test? Did they suspect that I was a phony?

I poured myself another cup of coffee and thought about Cornelius Braddigan. Or, more specifically, I thought about the day he hired me as the Braddigan Brothers security man. I showed up at his Pullman on time, but old Corny was nowhere to be found. The boss canvasman poked his grizzled head into the car and assured me that the owner of the circus would be along shortly. "You know how it is," the boss canvasman had said with a sigh. "There's always something that needs his attention." Meanwhile, my attention was drawn to a crisp twenty dollar bill, folded neatly in half on the carpet beneath Corny's chair. Assuming that it had fallen out of the drawer, I put it inside the desk.

That incident had faded from memory until my last day on the job, when Corny presented me with the very same twenty dollar bill as a token of his gratitude. I was about to tell him that a measly twenty bucks for twenty years of exemplary service not solving any crimes was hardly a token of gratitude when he explained that it he'd placed it on the floor of the Pullman as a test. "I lost sixty dollars that morning," he told me. "Weren't you curious about why I gave you the job? You were the only prospect who didn't pocket the bill."

Maybe this sort of thing was common in show business. What's the difference between a Borscht Belt resort and a circus, or a Broadway theatre and a carnival? Whether the skin is made of canvas or marble or the bones are made of poles or pillars, it's all the same heart that beats inside.

I had just managed to convince myself that Harry and Rina were putting me on when I heard a clatter outside. I leapt to my feet and ran out of the bungalow, and in the wan light of early morning I saw Rina Katz somnambulating across the frost-fringed grass in a state of undress that would've made a hoochie-coochie dancer blush. And just as suddenly as she had emerged from her bungalow she withdrew into it, all while completely asleep. *Of course!* That would explain her uncanny feeling that something was amiss in the office. *She had opened the safe and didn't even realize it!* But this unusual turn of events left me with another problem, and this was a problem that couldn't be solved as serendipitously: Where did she put the money?

As the morning brightened I got down on my hands and knees and studied the ground by the office door, self-conscious but grateful that Neetenin's lodgers were not early risers. In the damp soil I could see a set of footprints I recognized as my own, and another set of prints made by Rina's pumps, both from the night before. A third set of prints, made by bare feet, could have been made by Harry after he had roused me from my sleep, or by a sleepwalking Mrs. Katz. It was a cinch—or so I thought.

"Archie Newcomb?" boomed a voice I recognized as belonging to Johnny Murphy, the house dick for Kirshner's Hideaway. "Care to talk a walk?" he asked, adding that he wanted to discuss a burglary that had occurred at Kirshner's the week before. After telling me his story I had no choice but to exonerate Rina Katz.

* * * *

It was my evening off, and I cradled a sangaree at a table in the back of the packed room as I watched the great Yiddish comic, Julian Rose, put on his "Levinsky at the Wedding" routine. Julian, attired in top hat and tails with his signature white rose in his lapel, had just begun his bit about the bride and her bouquet of don'tcha-forget-it-nots when Harry and Rina joined me at the table with a couple of out-of-town friends visiting from Manhattan.

"Tell the Bombergs about how you caught that *gonif*," said Harry, after the comic had taken his bow to raucous applause. Suddenly I discovered how a second-rate vaudeville hoofer must feel taking the stage after a hot act. I humbly told the Bombergs that it was just a matter of studying the lodge register.

"When I talked to the detective from Kirshner's we compared notes about which acts had been booked at both resorts at the time of the robberies. There were only a few," I said, counting the acts on three fingers of my left hand— Lasky & Finkel, Green & Weber, and Molly Picon. The Bombergs gasped; perhaps they were imagining Picon, a waifish gamin, fiddling with the combination of a safe with a revolver tucked into her little boy britches.

"Upon reviewing the register, there was one name that caught my attention," I continued. "It was the road manager for Green and Weber, a young fellow by the name of Jackie Biltwright." The Bombergs sighed in unison, relieved that the culprit had been a gentile. A lousy amateur animal act took the stage, and I took advantage of this opportunity to lead the Bombergs on an impromptu tour of the Neetenin Lodge office. "Won't you follow me?" I asked. I poured the last of the sangaree down my throat and led the out-of-towners down the hallway, with Harry Katz on our heels.

"Why did that name ring a bell?" asked Mr. Bomberg. "A hardened criminal, is he?"

"Hardly," I said, opening the office door. The safe stood in a corner of the room. "In fact, his record is clean as a whistle. I telephoned the act's booking agent and asked if Jackie was from Duluth. When the agent said yes, I knew I had my man."

"How so?" asked Mrs. Bomberg. Harry pointed to the tiny metal tag bolted to the front of the heavy steel safe, and she squinted her eyes to read the inscription: *Bilt-Rite Manufacturing Co., Duluth, Minnesota.*

"His old man founded the company," I explained. "Years before Jackie went to college as a mechanical engineer. Say, Mrs. Bomberg, can I borrow one of your hairpins? Thank you. Now, I'm afraid I must ask the both of you to turn around."

A second later I had the safe open, thanks to a mechanical vulnerability that Mr. Biltwright's son had intentionally added to the design.

"When Jackie traded his drafting table for a route book, it was time for him to go out on the road and reap what he had planted ten years earlier," I said. "The kid would've gotten away with it, too, if only he hadn't forgotten the cardinal rule of show business: Never sign the guest register using your real name." Harry murmured in assent and the Bombergs nodded.

On the walk back to the dining room, I heard Mrs. Bomberg remark to her husband that, while she had enjoyed the story about the Neetenin Lodge robbery, she preferred "Levinsky at the Wedding." I couldn't argue with that critique; I suppose that's what I get for attempting to follow Julian Rose.

Marlin Bressi is the author of four nonfiction books, including *Hairy Men in Caves: True Stories of America's Most Colorful Hermits* (Sunbury Press, 2015), and *Pennsylvania Oddities* (Sunbury Press, 2018). His fiction has appeared in *Suspense Magazine, Mystery Tribune, Best New England Crime Stories*, Fresh Ink, Capsule Stories, and other publications.

THE FIRST ANNUAL ATCHAFALAYA COYOTE HUNT: OR, IS THERE A SLEUTH IN THE HOUSE

O'NEIL DE NOUX

I always wanted to be a sleuth. Pfft! As if.

Don't know why that came to mind as we made a sharp right turn, Ben slowing his British racing-green Chrysler through a stand of towering oaks lining either side of the road, live oaks with wide, gnarly branches hanging over the road like gigantic spider legs.

"Did I mention the hydraulic shock absorbers?" said Ben. "That's how we glide through curves."

Ben had detailed every aspect of his wonderful, new 1924 Chrysler model B-70 since we left New Orleans, nearly putting me to sleep after we crossed the Mississippi at Baton Rouge to roll across what he called *le flottant*—the great floating marsh-prairie between the Mississippi River and Texas over a hundred miles away. We moved, inexorably into the Atchafalaya River Basin.

"We're getting close," Ben announced.

I envisioned a dark castle at the end of the tunnel of oaks, picturing a brooding place with vacant, eye-like windows from the Edgar Allan Poe House of Usher story. At the end of the oaks, we turned left and the sky opened bright blue with billowy clouds and Ben eased off the blacktop to a wide white shell driveway leading to a huge, brilliant-white plantation house with six tall ionic columns in front. Fields of sugar cane stood to the right and an open meadow to the left and a forest of oaks and wide magnolia trees running to a vast expanse of piney woods and an even vaster expanse of cypress swamp beyond.

Ben parked between a red Duesenberg and a blue Stutz Bearcat. A footman materialized to carry Ben's gear, including his shotgun case. Blond-haired and blue-eyed Ben took my hand and straightened his back as he led me to the lawn in front of the plantation house. He moved on the balls of his feet to stay above my 5'10". Scents of gardenias and roses floated over us as we passed a garden.

Ben led me up ten brick steps to double doors standing open and into a marble foyer with men in riding outfits, a white banner hanging from the spiral staircase reading:

The First Annual Atchafalaya Coyote Hunt
Saturday, June 7, 1924

A man with a twin-lens camera snapped a photo of the banner, flash bulb popping.

"It appears we made it just in time," Ben said, letting go of my hand and moving to a long table to speak to a young woman who beamed up at him, stood and hurried around to hug him. I moved aside as four men carrying gun cases hurried past, two of them ogling me as they went by.

I knew I looked good. No Hollywood beauty but at twenty-five I've never looked better. Dark red hair from my mother's Irish side, straight nose, deep-set blue eyes from my father's English side. My shorter-than-fashion-allowed beaded dress hugged my curvy figure and my dark crimson lipstick accentuated my cupie-doll lips on my creamy white complexion.

Ben and the woman who hugged him came over and Ben introduced me to his second cousin once-removed Marietta Hart. He excused himself so he could change and get ready.

"Nice to meet you," I told Marietta.

"Charmed to meet you, Cher." Marietta pointed back to the table. "I have to git back."

Marietta returned to her table and I stepped through the foyer, past a huge double staircase into a ballroom, a library on the left and huge dining room on the right. I continued to a line of French doors opening to a large covered gallery at the back of the house, gallery supported by six more ionic columns. A couple dozen men stood on the wide lawn behind the house. Unlike the red-coated fox hunters back in England, these Americans wore khaki and green and brown to hunt coyotes. They did not appear aware canines were color-blind. No pageantry in khaki.

"You really from England, Cher?" Marietta had come up behind me. "You sound like y'all from England. You from London? Ben says you have a 'y' in your first name *an* last name."

"Yes." I spelled out Gwendolyne Wynter for her. "I am from Yorkshire." Cannot figure Marietta's accent. It wasn't southern and it wasn't the way Ben talked, like a New Yorker. He told me his was a New Orleans accent. More Brooklynese than Southern. Marietta's accent had almost a French lilt to it. Ben said his cousins were Cajun, descendants of the French who lost the French and Indian War and were expelled from Canada by the bloody British.

"I like y'all's dress. You a flapper?"

"No."

My dress did not reach my knees, like a flapper, but my hair flowed past my shoulders—my hair too pretty for me to bob—and I did not smoke, did not like to drink or dance that much. Maybe Ben told her how we'd met at a petting party. Making out but only light petting. Flappers did that. Like a good flapper I wore step-in French panties but Ben did not know that, unless he'd peeked up my skirt.

I said, "Ben tells me they released the three coyotes around dawn."

"Shush." Marietta pressed a finger against her lips. "Dat's a secret, Cher."

"He said they were brought in from Arizona. Haven't eaten for three days. No water for two days. And they are lost. Weak, confused, easy prey."

Ben had told me coyotes were few in Louisiana, all here west of the Mississippi.

"I asked Ben if there were wolves here and he said there were red wolves, smaller than the big wolves out west and too secretive to be found by hounds."

"Well, les just hope de hounds don stumble on a bobcat. Swamp cats round here are big an mean."

A group of men came out of the house to the gallery. The group stopped and two burly men in black suits and sunglasses escorted a tall man in a white tie and tails, black shoes shiny like glass, the man's white hair brighter than I'd ever seen. This must be our host, Ben's cousin Alexander Le Guerrier. The tall man moved to the center of the gallery and Ben eased around to stand next to me. He'd changed into a dark green jacket, khaki shirt and tan British riding pants we called jodhpurs, and tall brown boots, his double-barrel shotgun broken open and draped over his left arm.

The tall man spread his arms and said in a high-pitched voice, "Welcome. Welcome all. As mos a y'all know, I am yoar host Alexander Le Guerrier an today we begin a new tradition. A Coyote Hunt in Louisiana."

A clamoring turned me to the rear lawn where men in silk jockey outfits—purple with pink stripes, green with orange polka dots, blue stripes on maroon background—led a string of saddled horses.

"Y'all know de rules," Alexander waved toward the horses. "Mount up. De coyotes are loose."

Loud barking turned me to the right as three boys struggled to hold onto the leashes of about three dozen dogs. Now these were not British foxhounds, but American bloodhounds and beagles and German shepherds. A fourth boy scrambled into view leading a pack of Doberman pinchers. These Americans were hilarious.

Ben took my hand, squeezed it and said, "Wish me luck."

"Uhh."

He jogged off and found a black-and-white pony to climb on. Not a thoroughbred like back in England but a small horse, the size of moor pony. Someone blew a bugle, not the high-pitched horn of a fox hunt. It sounded like a cavalry charge in an American western movie.

The dogs were set loose, dragging their leashes as they raced off, the bloodhounds bellowing to the left, the beagles barking and racing to the right, the German shepherds scattering in different directions, the Dobermans fighting each other, biting and screeching as they rambled around the plantation house. A black-and-white cat raced from behind a bush and scrambled up an oak tree. The dogs did not notice.

"The men," I told Marietta, "Are you not worried? In khaki. They might shoot one another."

Marietta laughed. "So long as dey stay in front of de guns, dey will be safe. None of dem can shoot wurf a damn." She pointed to Alexander Le Guerrier. "He goes nowhere wifout his bodyguards, no."

We both watched the horsemen trying to catch up with the dogs.

"Dogs better stick togetta. A coyote got bigger teeth den a dog and come from a hostile environment. Better scrappers, don you tink? How bout a mint julip?"

Another jockey-clad man led a black carriage up to the Gallery. A man in a white lab coat stepped up to Alexander and handed the old man a thermos. He passed it to one of his bodyguards, while the other bodyguard helped him into the carriage. Marietta poked my side and nodded to the man in the white lab coat.

"Doctor Frankenstein. Real name—Dr. Franken. I'm not sure why dey call him Frankenstein. Somebody tole me it's from a scary book. He just check dat thermos for poison. He tests ereyting de old man drink and eat."

A bodyguard tucked a blanket around the old man's legs and Alexander pulled a long revolver from inside his coat and raised it high. The two black stallions led the carriage toward the piney woods with Alexander and his two bodyguards. They went the direction where the beagles had gone.

"Come along." Marietta grabbed my arm. "Mint Julips."

She led us inside to a side bar where an elderly man in a sky-blue tuxedo handed drinks to a young couple.

"Ouu." Marietta went. "Is dat Umpopa?"

"It sure is."

Marietta scooped up two tall glasses filled with bright-red liquid and shaved ice, passed one to me. She took a deep draft and smacked her lips. "Ah. Umpopa. Hab you ever had it?"

I shook my head, sniffed the drink and caught a hint of cinnamon. I asked the elderly man what was in it.

"Pomegranate juice and prune juice with gin, vodka, bitters, bingara, galunna extract, and sprinkles of nutmeg. And cinnamon."

I asked for an iced tea, a newly acquired taste since I came to America two years ago.

A group approached and Marietta touched my arm again.

"Ouu. Ouu." She called out to the approaching group. "Lemme introduce you to de girl Ben brought to dis soiree. Miss Gwendolyne Wynter of Yorktown, England."

"Yorkshire. I believe Yorktown is in Virginia."

The three men and two women stepped close.

Marietta announced, "Ben and dees tree men are Alexander Le Guerrier's closest relations." She leaned toward me and lowered her voice, "If the great man should succumb to anyting fatal, dey will be rich."

As opposed to succumbing to something non-fatal. These Americans were hilarious.

The nearest man stepped close with a whippet on a leash, the dog's tail wagging wildly. The man wore a blue suit, extended his hand to give me a damp handshake, "De name's Edward Le Guerrier."

Edward stood about 6'2", nice build with thinning blond hair, blue eyes, maybe forty years old. The second man, in a tan suit and named Pepper Le Guerrier, shook my hand with a firm grip. He was a little shorter, a little heavier, a little younger, also with thinning blond hair and blue eyes. The third man, in a dark green suit and named Darnell Le Guerrier, looked the youngest, early twenties, about 5'9", thick build, more blond hair and blue eyes.

The whippet came over to sniff my ankles.

"We're sisters," the woman in a red dress said. She pointed to the woman in a pink dress. "She is Mary and I'm Ann." She waved her hand around. "We have romances with de cousins, mais yeah."

Everyone talked at once and I sipped my iced tea, sweeter than I liked it. The men told me what they did—Darnell a lawyer in Baton Rouge, Pepper a realtor in some place called Opelousas, Edward a history professor at Tulane University in New Orleans.

"I hear dogs," Pepper said and the men hurried to the rear gallery.

Mary and Ann scooped up glasses of Umpopa. I brought my tea.

Marietta said, "Alexander Le Guerrier keep telling us he has no will so ereyting he own and all de money he got in banks in Baton Rouge and New Orleans will be divided equally between his closest relations."

Among.

"Dat's how Louisiana law work. No will. De wealt divided among living relations."

"He did it so no one will get it all," Mary said.

"No incentive to kill de old fool," Ann said. "But he gonna die eventually."

"It will be a natural death," Marietta said. "He too careful to get killed by anyone."

Mary said, "He could fall out of de carriage."

"He could have a secret will," I said and they fell silent.

Someone whooped outside and dogs barked louder. A gunshot echoed and Marietta led the sisters to the gallery with me trailing. We stopped as we stepped out on the gallery to watch the pack of Dobermans barking and snarling as they fought each other crossing behind the gallery. Edward's whippet whimpered, hid behind its master. For a moment, it looked like the Dobermans would head our way and Marietta shouted for us to come in and shut the French doors. Before we did, the dogs turned and raced away, chasing each other toward the cane fields.

Gunfire echoed in the distance.

I smelled the food now. The main reason I came. Ben promised a Cajun and Creole feast of exotic dishes—filé gumbo with chicken, crawfish bisque, shrimp etouffeé, jambalaya, fried shrimp, fried oysters, blackened redfish, and two sausages whose names I'd memorized—andouille and boudin. Men in white chef hats moved from the plantation house to a white building.

Marietta must have seen me looking at the building and said, "De big kitchen."

Two riders rode up, one with a carcass over his saddle. Three men in tuxes stepped out to greet them and the man with the carcass dropped it on the lawn next to the gallery, not far from us.

"Judges," Marietta explained as the three men in tuxes stepped close to the carcass. The oldest shook his head.

"Jeanfreau. You shot dis?"

"Mais yeah. One coyote down."

"You moron. Dat's no coyote. Dat's a yellow dog. It has a collar on it. You shot somebody's dog."

"Stupid ass," a second judge said. "Dis is too chunky to be a coyote. Dey skinny as hell."

"Emaciated," said the third judge while the oldest judge stepped down to check the dead dog's collar.

"Pettigrew. You shot Com Pettigrew's dog, you fool."

That drew chuckles.

The two riders took off back to the woods, two footmen carried off the dead dog, and the three judges went back into the plantation house.

"I'll check on de vittles." Darnell shuffled toward the big kitchen.

Wonderful smells wafted our way making my stomach grumble.

"Is dat one of de coyotes?" Pepper pointed to a streaking canine racing out of the cane fields and heading straight for us.

Edward's whippet whined and pulled at its leash. The black carriage approached from the other direction, out of the woods and headed our way. The streaking canine came closer and barked.

German shepherd.

The whippet jumped into Edward's arms. The German shepherd raced past the plantation house without slowing. Edward put the whippet down and it ran into the plantation house. The carriage arrived, horses snorting. The two bodyguards climbed down and Alexander stood and called out, "I heard dey shot one."

No one answered so I told him they'd shot a yellow dog. Had a collar. Belonged to someone named Pettigrew. The others ducked away. Alexander glared at me. He'd acquired a pair of tan riding gloves.

"Who are you?"

"I'm Ben's date." I smiled.

"Pettigrew? Com Pettigrew's dog?"

"Seems that way."

He looked back at the woods, wiped his brow with a gloved hand, wiped his mouth with the other and pulled off the gloves, dropped them into the carriage. A bodyguard helped him down. The old man stood stiffly, tugged on his tuxedo coat and came my way. He stepped up on the gallery, moved to me, stopped and covered his mouth with a hand and coughed. He coughed again, took a step back, hands falling to his side. Spittle dripped from his mouth. He rocked on his heels, foam gurgling in his mouth and his eyes rolled back and he collapsed.

I've never had that effect on any man. Maybe a little spittle.

Alexander's left foot quivered and his back arched and stiffened.

"Dr. Franken!" Marietta called back to the Plantation House while the two bodyguards knelt next to Alexander, one picking up a wrist the other pressing fingers against the prone man's throat. We stepped aside as Dr. Franken rushed out. He went down on his knees to check Alexander. Everyone backed away.

The doctor stood and said, "Poisoned."

He looked at the two bodyguards. "What did he consume?"

"Nothing."

"He did not even drink from the thermos." These men had no Cajun accent. Imported talent, no doubt. Sounded like Ben's accent.

A crowd gathered behind us. The doctor asked someone to fetch the sheriff.

Marietta grabbed my arm. "Oh, no."

Thought she was going to say something about dead Alexander but she said, "Wait 'til get a load of Sheriff Deserved Parker."

The suspense was short-lived as a big man in a black suit and wearing a white derby came out of the plantation house and stepped up to the body. I'd never seen a white derby before.

"Fill me in, Doc."

The doctor filled him in, the sheriff raising a hand to stop him in mid-explanation, bellowed, "We have to seal off de area." He turned to a man in a khaki uniform.

"Deputy, call out de posse."

"Posse?"

"Ereyone. Whole damn department. Put out one of dem all-point-tings and call Iberville Parish Sheriff's Office and Iberia Parish, Lafayette Parish, Saint Landry Parish, and Pointe Coupee Parish. Tell all a dem Alexander Le Guerrier been murdered, yeah. We need hep."

The whippet raced out of the plantation house and jumped into the carriage. It snapped both riding gloves in its mouth, jumped down and raced back to Edward and dropped them. The dog stood wagging its tail and panting, let out a low growl, spittle flying from its mouth. He let out a cry, foaming at the mouth and collapsed.

"How de hell did dat happen?"

I waited for it but it didn't come. Everyone just looked at the dog. Except Edward, who began to back away.

"The poison is on the gloves," I said.

"How you know dat?" The sheriff said, taking off his derby to reveal a bald head.

"History." I pointed to Edward, the history professor from Tulane. "He can tell you. And that's his whippet. Bringing the gloves back to his master."

Edward turned and ran into the plantation house.

The sheriff shoved his deputy. "Well, go get 'im." The sheriff stepped close to me, said, "How'd you figure dis out, little filly?"

"I'm not a little filly. As you can tell from my accent, I'm from England and anyone with a rudimentary knowledge of English history knows the legend of Duke Conan II. A man so afraid of being poisoned he had all his food tested before he ate. He was done in by William the Conqueror who had poison rubbed on Conan's riding gloves so when the man wiped his mouth, the poison was administered. Edward teaches history at Tulane. He has to know the story."

The sheriff put his hat back on, straightened his back.

"Well, damn," he said.

And I thought—*maybe I am a sleuth after all. Pfft!*

"Makes sense to me," Marietta said. "Edward's been having money problems. Too impatient to wait for de old man to kick off."

A half dozen riders approached, including Ben, the only one to come straight to the gallery. He reigned his horse and looked at me and asked, "Did I miss anything?"

O'Neil De Noux has 43 books published, more than 400 short story sales and a screenplay produced in 2000. He's published in genres including historical fiction, children's fiction, mainstream, mystery, science-fiction, suspense, fantasy, horror, western, literary, religious, romance, erotica, and humor. Writing awards: the Shamus Award twice, the Derringer Award and Police Book of the Year (awarded by PoliceWriters.com). Two of his stories have been in the *Best American Mystery Stories* annual anthology (2003 and 2013).

A REMOTE CHANCE

DAVID RUDD

The Annual Crime Writers Convention of 2008, held in Bristol, UK, was probably the most celebrated in that organization's history, being the last one to be attended by the infamous American crime writer, Miles Freeman. It was not just Freeman's final appearance there but anywhere, as his body, with a gun beside it, was discovered, by a maid, in his locked hotel room. The set-up sounded like something straight out of a game of *Cluedo*, as though the man were enacting one of his own murder mysteries. But, given the man's reputation, his death caused quite a stir.

Freeman had always been a larger-than-life character, game for acting out the plots of his own stories. His penchant for these performances was said to originate in his carny background, though how much was true of what he told the public, is another matter. He was certainly renowned for his stunts: escaping locked containers, being buried alive, walking across pits of fire and so on. He was even said to try out well-known poisons on himself, gauging their effects and symptoms. Some of you, in fact, might remember his infamous appearance on Graham Norton's chat show, where he was unable to stop shaking, his skin a cyanotic blue as a result of some toxin he'd ingested. He had claimed that he could cure himself by bloodletting, and then proceeded to take a blade to his forearm. You could see the other guests squealing and cringing, but the procedure did seem to restore Freeman to a healthy color.

As a result of this reputation, many initially viewed Freeman's demise as simply another stunt and were awaiting the news that he had recovered and was now heartily breakfasting in the hotel restaurant. After all, hadn't he once been buried alive in a sarcophagus for ten hours? Consequently, most of the convention delegates readily agreed to have their fingerprints taken, when asked, going along with what they thought was another of Freeman's exploits.

It took people quite a while to adjust to the fact that Freeman really was dead and that, in the middle of their Convention, a murder enquiry was taking place. By that afternoon, Romulus Carson, renowned for his own locked-room mysteries, had become the main suspect, although many delegates found it inconceivable that Carson—whose day job was Professor of Early English Literature at Keble College, Oxford—could have "dunnit." He was such an upright, fastidious man, despite the intense rivalry that existed between the two writers. It was well known by delegates that each had won the prestigious Platinum Dagger Award twice, making 2008 a key year for their play-off—presuming that another author didn't scoop the prize.

Given that the set-up sounded more like a suicide, with Freeman's body in the locked room, how had Carson become implicated? Actually, it was something quite basic: Carson's prints were all over the gun. Even so, Carson's interrogation by the police did not last long. He was quickly able to convince them of the error of their ways.

"If I had committed this crime," he had said, "would I leave the weapon, with *my* prints all over it, right next to Freeman's body?"

"Well, sir—"

"Don't you think I might have tried to dispose of the gun?"

"You might have wanted it to look like suicide."

"With my prints all over it? At the very least, wouldn't I have wiped the weapon, placed it in Freeman's hand...?"

Detective Inspector Arthur Cumberson, in charge of the case, realized he was getting nowhere. He had always thought Carson an unlikely suspect, but the presence of his prints made the interview a necessity.

"So, how *do* you explain your prints on the gun?" asked Cumberson.

"Simple. It's my weapon."

Cumberson was dumbfounded. How typical of a crime writer, the detective inspector later told his team, to hold back on such a key piece of information.

It turned out that Carson had brought his gun to the previous year's Crime Convention, where he had used it in a ballistics demonstration. Afterwards, the gun had disappeared—obviously pinched by someone who, as Carson argued, was present again this year: someone who wanted to pin Freeman's death on him. And, as Carson added, he wouldn't put it past Freeman himself to have pulled such a stunt.

It was a credible hypothesis but, as Cumberson pointed out to his SOCO (Scene of Crime Officer) team, no one would go to the lengths of killing himself simply to exact revenge. Clearly, if Freeman had planned something along these lines, the stunt had gone badly wrong.

Cumberson now felt he had earned himself one of the hotel restaurant's full English breakfasts, but he had no sooner begun to enjoy it than Dr. William Grosvenor, the forensic scientist on the team, headed over to him.

For his part, Grosvenor knew that they'd not got off to a good start. He'd made the mistake of thinking that Cumberson would get the cultural reference when he introduced his team as "CSI operatives," adopting not only the American term, but also putting on an exaggerated American accent (his own was Glaswegian). He and his team had then made matters worse by exchanging choice snatches of dialog from the TV show that had featured Freeman's hip detective, Alonso Palmari. Cumberson had still not twigged the source of their in-jokes; in fact, he'd objected strongly, especially when they referred to the local pathologist as a "carver of cadavers."

Cumberson had walked off in high dudgeon, muttering, "Bit of respect!"

Grosvenor, keen to build bridges, this time adopted a more formal, deferential approach to the DI. "I've just had an initial report from the path lab, sir," he began. "Would you like me to wait till you've breakfasted?"

Cumberson, mouth bulging, shook his head. He gestured to the seat opposite, which Grosvenor took.

"Apparently," said Grosvenor, stealing himself to stick to the facts, "Freeman had recently had a cholecystectomy."

Immediately he'd said it, he could see it was a mistake. "What the hell does that mean?" spluttered the DI. "Can't you speak plain English?"

"No, I'm Scottish, ya humorless wanker!" Grosvenor had wanted to say, but curbed himself. "We'll have the fuller picture when we get Freeman's medical records but, basically, it means he'd had his gall bladder removed. It's a fairly common treatment for gallstone sufferers. The bullet was found where the gall bladder would normally have been located. But"—Grosvenor paused, waiting politely for Cumberson to stop chewing—"it seems that the bullet itself had been there a good while. Months, in fact. It's become embedded in the surrounding soft tissue."

"Are we saying that this bullet *didn't* kill him?"

"Indeed, sir."

"But what about all the blood and mess where a bullet seems to have penetrated?"

"Well, that's very intriguing, sir. According to the pathologist, Dr. Ramsey, the torn flesh and, indeed, the matching holes in Freeman's trousers and underwear, all seem to have been made by a blade of some sort."

Cumberson looked suitably shocked.

"And that's not all," Grosvenor continued, relaxing into this new persona. "Though it's thought that the bullet came from Carson's gun, it seems that the weapon itself had not been fired recently, and certainly not within the last twelve hours, when Freeman's death must have occurred."

He watched Cumberson with fascination. The man seemed to be poking down his food ever faster. Did a "full English" eventually turn its consumer into something fully English? he wondered. If so, he'd avoid it.

"So, I asked myself," concluded Grosvenor, "if it wasn't the projectile itself, what was the mechanism of Freeman's death?"

Cumberson waited for Grosvenor to continue but, unlike earlier, the silence dragged on. He looked up impatiently. "Well, man," he snapped, "What 'mechanism' was it?"

"Sorry, sir." Grosvenor had been miles away. Cumberson's rhythmic chomping had mesmerized him. As the DI stoked forkful after forkful down his gullet, Grosvenor had almost pictured himself reporting Cumberson's demise, not Freeman's: blocked arteries leading to a fatal stroke, he wanted to caution the DI.

He refocused: "Mortality, sir, a result of exsanguination from a stab wound."

That halted him, mid-chew. "Ex-sang-wi-nation?" Cumberson spread the syllables with deliberation. "Do you mean," Cumberson stabbed at the yolk of his second egg, "he bled to death?"

"Indeed, sir."

"Was it self-inflicted or did someone…?" Grosvenor watched the yolk pooling on the DI's plate as the man simulated stabbing movements with his dripping knife, "attack him?"

"Without the weapon itself—the knife or whatever it was—it's difficult to say. The angle makes it possible for Freeman to have done it himself, though why on earth he'd want to—"

"Freeman *was* known as the Human Pincushion, wasn't he?" pointed out Cumberson.

"That makes his bleeding to death all the more peculiar," replied Grosvenor. "You'd have expected such a man to have had more…more physiological control. On the other hand, given that he had that bullet lodged next to his liver, it would have been difficult for anyone else to stab him with such precision. That is, aligning the entry wound with the embedded slug."

"So, it looks as though we're still talking suicide, but dressed up to look like murder? Trying, perhaps, to implicate his old adversary, Carson?"

"It would seem so," said Grosvenor. "There's a very similar scene in one of Carson's novels, *The Cliftonville Murders*, where a body is arranged to look like a suicide, with a gun alongside it carrying someone else's prints."

"A fan of detective fiction, are we?" asked Cumberson.

"Indeed, sir. And film, sir—as me and the boys demonstrated earlier." He looked at the DI, hoping for some token of understanding. Nothing. "I couldna' believe my luck when I was assigned this case. To be in the company of so many famous authors."

Cumberson groaned. "Why is it that each of these amateurs thinks they can do a better job than the people who have real expertise in dealing with murders?"

Grosvenor decided not to admit that he, too, was an amateur crime writer. Cumberson went back to his congealing fry-up, mopping up the yolk with some thickly buttered bread.

"I'll get back to Freeman's room, then," said Grosvenor.

"Get the team to search it thoroughly," Cumberson shouted after him. "From what you say, we need to find a blade."

"Yes sir." Grosvenor made the mistake of looking back, in time to witness the man's pink tongue enthusiastically cleaning his knife.

* * * *

That evening, Grosvenor once again sought out Cumberson, whom he found in their makeshift incident room.

"Good God, man!" exclaimed Cumberson, when he caught sight of the forensic scientist. "What's wrong with your arm?" Grosvenor's left forearm had swollen up like a balloon.

In reply, Grosvenor held out a plastic container. Cumberson couldn't help but blanch at the sight of the huge black spider within. Spiders were the one thing he couldn't handle in any rational way. Grosvenor spotted his discomfort.

"A Sydney funnel-web, sir. But you needn't worry. Most of its toxins," he waved his arm in the air, "are safely in here!"

"I'm sure he's a very impressive specimen," Cumberson managed to say, wondering how the man could be so flippant. "Sidney, you say?"

"Yes, sir. From Australia: a Sydney funnel-web. I was looking for evidence of poisons and found him in a drawer. Or, rather," again he waved his arm theatrically, "he found me!"

Cumberson did not look amused. "So, are you saying that this Sidney was planted?"

"Exactly. He's not from round here… Sydney, in fact."

Fortunately, as Grosvenor now explained, he had had ready access to an anti-toxin, which he'd taken before the muscle spasms had become too excruciating. Cumberson, grimacing, watched Grosvenor as he probed his arm with what seemed a morbid enthusiasm.

"Had Freeman been stung, then?" asked Cumberson.

"Bitten, sir," quietly corrected Grosvenor.

"He'd been bitten!"

"No, sir. *Not* bitten, although that's what this spider does." Grosvenor once again waved his arm. "It's a bit like the gun, sir. There's the *presence* of a weapon, but it's not been used."

Grosvenor hesitated a moment. "We did find one, curious puncture mark on Freeman's right thumb, but it's certainly no' a bite—unlike these things!" Once again, Grosvenor probed the inflamed perforations on his arm.

"We'll soon know exactly what was in his system," continued Grosvenor. "The boys in toxicology are onto it." Grosvenor turned to leave, then stopped. "Oh, when one of the delegates spotted my arm, she pointed me towards this." Grosvenor held up a book.

"*Come into My Parlor* by Bobby Horner," read Cumberson. "The title's certainly suggestive."

"Yes, Horner's an Australian who often features deadly arachnids in his stories, alongside other noxious fauna. This one involves a locked room, too."

"And you think that Freeman might have planted Sidney, copying yet another whodunnit plot?"

"Well, the cap certainly fits, sir, and, as I've just learned, Horner also had an altercation with Freeman—in fact, a punch-up—at last year's convention. Like Carson, Horner too accused Freeman of filching ideas."

"So, you think that Horner could be someone else that Freeman wanted to implicate in his dastardly web?"

"Oh, very good sir!" said Grosvenor. Cumberson looked perplexed. Grosvenor started to explain the DI's metaphorical use of the word "web," but Cumberson waved him away.

Grosvenor returned to Freeman's room, where the two other members of the SOCO team, Rob and Pete, were togged up in their protective clothing, undertaking an exhaustive search.

"Anything else of interest, guys?" asked Grosvenor, as he started pulling on his own gear.

"Not really—there's his bedside reading." Pete gestured to three novels on the table. As Grosvenor idly picked up the top volume, Pete added, "Which I've not yet checked for prints."

"Oops!" said Grosvenor, still without his gloves on. He was glad Cumberson wasn't around.

The top novel was Carson's *The Cliftonville Murders*. Horner's *Come into my Parlor* was also there. "Another deliberate clue, eh guys?" said Grosvenor. The third book, he noted with interest, was a novel by Hermione Threadgold called *Hotel Hotspot*. He flicked through it.

"It's years since I read this," he went on, "but I have a feeling it involves poison of some sort." He looked up to see that Pete and Rob were both ignoring him, intent on their search. After a few more minutes riffling through the pages, though, Grosvenor became more animated: "Aye, that's it! Rob?" The SOCO caught his eye. "Ice-cubes in the mini-bar. Can we get them checked out?"

Rob nodded and retrieved the tray from the minibar. He carefully labelled it and packed it into a cold box.

Grosvenor tried to avoid interrupting them anymore. He idly pulled open the drawer that had contained "Sidney," as he would always think of that funnel-web spider in future. As though anticipating some of the arachnid's relatives, he moved slowly. Then he spotted a TV remote tucked in at the back. He'd normally have ignored such an everyday object but…hadn't he just seen another remote over by the TV? He looked across. Yes, there it was.

Why two? he found himself asking. He pointed the one from the drawer at the TV and pressed a button. The screen sprang to life. Grosvenor quickly turned it off and grabbed the other remote, the one over by the TV. He shook it. Could it, perhaps, conceal a missing blade? Nothing rattled. He then pointed it at the screen and pressed the button. The TV remained silent but Grosvenor himself let out a yell: "Ouch!"

Pete and Rob came across to see what he was complaining about this time. They had been present when the spider had attacked Grosvenor and were grateful to him for finding the beast before they did. They were equally appreciative now as the two watched Grosvenor, armed with a pair of tweezers, gingerly depress the rubberized button on the remote. As the button went down, the point of a small syringe emerged.

"Ouch!" echoed Rob, in sympathy.

Grosvenor then recalled the pinprick on Freeman's thumb. What had been in this needle? he wondered. He passed the device to Rob. "Open it up, can you?"

"Shouldn't we have checked it, too, for prints?" Pete once again interjected.

Grosvenor looked down at his right hand, still ungloved. "Perhaps we'll no' mention this to the DI?" he suggested.

Rob simply laughed and snapped open the device. Inside was a neat hydraulic mechanism, with a small, empty phial at one end.

"The question is," remarked Pete, "was that phial empty *before* you pressed the button, or only afterwards?"

"You certainly don't need any *more* toxins!" added Rob.

Grosvenor looked uneasy for a moment, shaking his arm tentatively. Then he smiled. "I'm good," he proclaimed.

He went back to Cumberson to report his findings, not only about the remote but also about the presence of those three novels in Freeman's room, which seemed to confirm Grosvenor's hunch that the writer had drawn on the plot of each to stage his demise. Grosvenor had then returned to the lab to have the remote checked for toxins and prints. He realized he'd probably destroyed the key print that might have been on the central "OK" button.

When he returned the following day, Cumberson had interviewed the two other authors, Horner and Threadgold, having already spoken to Carson. Each had confirmed their run-in with Freeman. Whereas Horner's had been a straight-forward punch-up, Threadgold's was more of a slow burner, beginning with an exchange of emails in which she'd complained about Freeman's shameless pla-giarism, resulting in the two of them having a disagreement on stage at last year's convention. It had ended with Threadgold stalking off, shouting "Thief!"

According to Cumberson, she had expressed no emotion over Freeman's death, which, to Threadgold, had seemed an entirely fitting end. "The man lived by the sword, so...," she had left her sentence unfinished, so Cumberson informed him. "And speaking of swords," he went on, "any more on that blade?"

Grosvenor was in middle of shaking his head when Pete arrived, beaming. "The Mystery of the Missing Blade ... solved!" he announced.

"Don't *you* start with the literary talk," grumbled Cumberson. He was becoming increasingly antipathetic to crime writers, acting, thought Grosvenor, as though he were a whodunnit victim trapped inside a locked room at the mercy of a bunch of writers' twisted imaginations.

Once Cumberson had quieted down, Pete updated him. Apparently, Free-man's daughter had arrived at the mortuary to pay her respects. On being shown her father's effects, she had picked up his copper bangle, which he had worn for his arthritis, and popped open one of its sections to reveal a small, pointed blade. According to her, everyone had seen it on the Graham Norton Show, where he'd used it on his arm. The clip, she said, was readily available on YouTube. The four men exchanged sheepish glances.

As for the bangle itself, Pete informed them, it had now been sent off to the path lab. "And there's more," concluded Pete, handing Grosvenor a printout of the findings from toxicology.

After studying them a while, Grosvenor shared the results with the others. "This is bizarre," he began. "The whole plastic pack of ice cubes had been con-taminated with a poison called antimycin, the one that features in Threadgold's novel. But the pack itself has not been opened, and there's no trace of antimycin in Freeman's system."

"A bit like Sidney the spider, then," said Cumberson. "A potential hazard only."

"Like Carson's gun, too," replied Grosvenor, "which also didn't kill him!"

"Despite the bullet in his innards," Pete added.

"But," Grosvenor had been reading on, "there *is* another toxin that's present in Freeman's system: *conium maculatum*, more commonly known as—"

"Hemlock," Rob finished his sentence for him.

"And where did that come from," asked Cumberson, "if not the ice cubes?" Grosvenor held up his pinpricked thumb.

"Ah yes," said Cumberson. "That TV remote." After a moment, he added: "I don't suppose there's anything about a 'spiked' remote in any of these whodunnits?"

Grosvenor shook his head. "Did we," asked Grosvenor, changing the subject, "get access to Freeman's computer, by the way?"

"Yes, it's still in our incident room," said Pete. "I don't think anyone's examined it yet."

"I'd like to have a look at that email exchange between Freeman and Threadgold," said Grosvenor. "If Freeman didn't delete it, that is. See if there are any clues there."

Cumberson waved him on his way, but Pete stopped him before he reached the door. "Shall we fingerprint it first?" Pete suggested. Grosvenor smiled.

* * * *

It was afternoon before Cumberson, Grosvenor, Pete and Rob met up again. They pooled their intelligence. Grosvenor had finally been sent a copy of Freeman's medical records, which he'd printed off. They confirmed that Freeman's gall bladder had been removed after an advanced carcinoma had been discovered, which, unfortunately, had already spread to his liver. According to these notes, Freeman had been given only a year to live—and this was written ten months ago. The cholecystectomy itself had been performed at a private clinic in Switzerland.

"I think," said Grosvenor, "that Freeman must have paid someone there to implant that bullet. So that's probably when he hatched the plan to stage this stunt: his supposed murder."

"The emphasis is on 'supposed', of course," stressed Cumberson, "for Freeman never *actually* intended to kill himself, did he? The cancer was doing that for him. But then his plan to implicate others seems to have backfired."

"I agree," said Grosvenor. "I'm guessing he was planning to do something more dramatic with that poison and…er, with Sidney, too. But he never got around to using them. He'd started with the bullet stunt, then misjudged things… bleeding to death."

"I still find it strange that someone like him," said Cumberson, echoing Grosvenor's earlier words, "someone who'd cut himself so often, should make such a basic error…. And," he added after a pause, "if he was pinching ideas from other people's stories, where's the one that features a barbed TV remote?"

"Perhaps he had an original idea for once," suggested Rob. There were some chuckles at this.

"What we do agree on," Grosvenor said, "is that Freeman had some involvement with each of these potential murder weapons—if we can call a spider a weapon. His prints were certainly on the pack of ice, and on the container that was used to transport Sidney the spider."

"And, of course, there were some prints on the remote, too," Pete added, "although they were somewhat compromised."

Grosvenor was about to apologize to Cumberson for this, and he was also toying with the idea of informing them about something else he'd uncovered. However, at that moment the DI launched into his summing up.

"So, it seems, lads," he said, "that we can safely say that Freeman *did* commit suicide, realizing that his time was almost up. But he thought he'd go out with a bang by trying to create one last locked-room mystery—and implicate his most voluble critics, too, by using their very own murder plots. Are we agreed?" Cumberson looked round at the SOCO team as each nodded in turn.

This was what Grosvenor wanted to hear. He now felt justified in keeping quiet, as he had about deleting some emails from Freeman's computer. They could always be recovered, of course, but he doubted anyone would bother checking. He knew that Freeman had been deliberately taunting them with that email trace, a trace that involved one more writer, as yet unnamed. It didn't really make much difference to the enquiry, did it? Grosvenor had almost convinced himself that this was so.

* * * *

As they sat together in the bar, enjoying a final beer, Grosvenor once again considered sharing his recent discovery: a brief email exchange between the deceased and a fairly new writer of crime fiction, Gerald Critchlow, someone whom Grosvenor rated highly. This exchange was far more interesting than the rather tedious spat that Freeman had had with Threadgold.

From what Grosvenor had read, it seemed that one of Critchlow's stories had been rejected by an anonymous reviewer because, so this reviewer argued, the idea of a syringe concealed inside a remote was too far-fetched. When Critchlow had challenged this verdict, the reviewer—Freeman, of course—had forsaken his cloak of anonymity in order to inform Critchlow, quite bluntly, that his idea would never work. Critchlow had responded with what now sounded like prescient words: "Not only will it work, but I'm convinced that, one day, you yourself will use it."

Critchlow's words rang relentlessly in Grosvenor's head. In his own mind, Grosvenor was convinced that Critchlow had only meant to give Freeman a shock, injecting him with just enough hemlock to paralyze him for a short time: to make the man realize that he'd been wrong to say such an idea wouldn't work. In fact, Grosvenor thought he could almost picture Freeman's reaction as he grudgingly acknowledged Critchlow as a worthy peer. "Gerald Critchlow, you old dog!" he might have said.

But, as Grosvenor also realized, had Freeman not said it fairly swiftly, he'd have found himself tongue-tied—completely immobilized, in fact. Then again, had Freeman not been engaged in his own nefarious schemes, Critchlow's stunt would have had a fairly innocuous outcome.

As it was, Freeman must have found himself in quite a predicament. He would, surmised Grosvenor, have used his concealed blade to create that wound in his side, leading to the bullet embedded next to his liver. He'd have been bleeding extensively but, before he could staunch the flow—something he'd normally have done with ease—he'd have found himself helpless, watching his life draining away. He couldn't even have scrawled an explanatory note declaring, "It was Critchlow wot dunnit."

As Grosvenor thought this through, he suddenly realized why Freeman would have turned on the TV just before he cut himself: it would have been to cover up any untoward cries he might emit.

With this final piece of the jigsaw, the whole crime scene now made sense. However, Grosvenor could still not come to terms with how regrettable such a sequence of events was. How remote were the chances? he wondered, then smiled to himself as the aptness of that phrase sank in: a remote chance, all right!

* * * *

The coroner's verdict was, indeed, suicide, which, some suggested, might have skewed the final decision of the Crime Writers Convention, awarding the Platinum Dagger to Freeman, albeit posthumously. Quite a few of the delegates were incensed at this decision. Not only had the man plagiarized them while alive, but his malign influence seemed to reach beyond the grave. People were even more incensed when they discovered that, anticipating victory, Freeman had already written a self-congratulatory acceptance speech, which was read out at the ceremony. And the final nail in their collective coffin was the healthy boost in Freeman's book sales as a result of the huge publicity that his bizarre death attracted.

* * * *

At the following year's event, this time held in Miami, it was a very different outcome, with a rank outsider winning the award: a forensic scientist who wrote under a pseudonym. He, though, was far more magnanimous in his acceptance speech, giving a special thank you to an inspirational Detective Inspector, and to Gerald Critchlow, in gratitude for his encouragement and what the winner termed his "expert insider knowledge."

✗

Dr. David Rudd is an emeritus professor of literature who turned out academic books and articles for some 40 years but always had a yearning to give his imagination freer rein. His stories have appeared in *Horla, TigerShark, Bandit Fiction, Literally Stories, The Creative Webzine, Jerry Jazz Musician, Erotic Review* and a Didcot Writers anthology, *First Contact*.

MINERVA JAMES AND THE HOUNDS OF HADES

MARK BRUCE

I strolled into Minerva James' law office on L Street in Sacramento one sunny morning in June 1962 to give my report on the murder of Johnny Hades, a local bordello owner. I stopped in the doorway. A little girl sat in Minerva's executive chair at Minerva's enormous desk. She had the same short curly black hair and patrician nose as the Boss. She wielded her crayons on a coloring book with the intensity of a diplomat signing the Treaty of Versailles.

"My daughter Aphrodite," Minerva said. She was standing by the window. "Di, this is my investigator, Carson Robinson." The little girl looked up at me solemnly, then flashed a brilliant smile. Her eyes were the color of a deep ocean on a sunny day. Then she went back to her coloring book. Woe to the young men who one day would be ensnared with that smile and those eyes!

"Your daughter?" I asked, trying not to look astonished.

"A souvenir of the War."

Minerva had previously told me that she'd been a nurse in a MASH unit during Korea. She hadn't mentioned a souvenir.

"You are no doubt wondering why a child is sitting and coloring at my desk on a weekday morning," Minerva said.

"Trouble at school?" I guessed.

"You are as perceptive as ever," Minerva said. "Di is far too intelligent to tolerate the snail's pace of learning in Public School. So, I am forced to send her to Catholic school."

"I didn't know you were Catholic," I said.

Minerva raised a dark eyebrow.

"I didn't say that," she said. "Di responds well to the nuns' academic rigor and discipline."

"Okay," I said, "except today, evidently. What did she do? Throw rocks through a stained-glass window?"

Minerva gave me a penetrating gaze.

"In a manner of speaking, that's exactly what she did. Her teacher assigned the class an essay, 'The Virgin Mary, Help in Troubled Times.'"

"I'm guessing Aphrodite's essay was not the personal spiritual document the nuns were looking for," I said.

Minerva walked over to her daughter. The boss was in her pearl business skirt and dark blue blouse. The girl was still in her St. Francis green plaid school uniform.

"Aphrodite," the boss continued, "chose to write about how the worship of the Virgin Mary is rooted in the ancient Greeks' devotions to the Goddess Athena. Complete with footnotes on her sources."

"Athena?" I said. "Isn't that the goddess the Romans called—"

"Minerva, yes," the boss said. The ghost of a smile flashed on her lips. Her daughter stole a glance at her mother with the same brief conspiratorial smile. Then she went back to her coloring.

"Why can't her father take her today?" I said.

Minerva gently rubbed a tuft of the girl's curly black hair between two slim white fingers. A look of unutterable sadness crossed her face.

"Her father is in Arlington," she said quietly.

At first, I thought she was saying the man was out of town. Then I realized what she meant: Arlington National Cemetery.

"As I said," Minerva murmured. "A souvenir of the war."

I nodded and said nothing. Minerva sat down in one of her visitor's chairs and motioned me to sit in the other.

"Tell me of the demimonde," she said, her voice attempting a lighter tone.

"The—uh, oh, Johnny Hades and Venus."

"Our client's name, I believe, is Delores Harrison," Minerva said in a chastising tone.

"Of course," I said. "It's just that I've been talking to people in a neighborhood where every woman seems to have a nickname. They all call her Venus."

I looked over at the child. Aphrodite, of course, was the Greek Goddess of Love. The Romans called her Venus.

"And Mr. Hades," Minerva said. "I believe his true name was Johnny Castro."

"Yes," I said, referring to my notebook.

"But I can see why one would want a new name in this particular neighborhood. Considering the business in which they were engaged," the boss said.

"True," I said, hesitantly. What I needed to tell Minerva was not for a child's ears.

Minerva saw me look over at Aphrodite. She released a small laugh that sounded like songbirds discussing Kant.

"Do not forbear because of Di," she said. "She's a defense lawyer's daughter. Sex and death are dinner table conversation."

Little Aphrodite continued to concentrate on her coloring, but I had the impression that her fingers clutching her sky-blue crayon slowed as I began my report.

Johnny Hades née Castro trafficked in flesh. He had a team (his term) of five women who provided companionship and comfort to lonely men. Also, sex.

For the most part, his girls told me, Johnny was good to them. He let them keep a quarter of what they earned (most pimps would take it all). He gave them a nice place to ply their trade (an apartment house he owned). He gave each of them personal attention which kept them sweet on him.

But, as one of Johnny's girls told me, "You don't want to hold out on Johnny. He always knows how many men you entertained and how much they paid. No skimming off the top or you got your ass beat."

Our client, Delores Harrison, was eighteen, barely. She'd run away from her wealthy Auburn family when she was seventeen but only got as far as Robertson Avenue near the trainyards in Sacramento. Johnny took her in, gave her a steady job, treated her nicely.

After a year in Johnny's employ, our client began to regret her choices. She had a wealthy family that would probably take her back in. She tried to run back home with the day's receipts once or twice. Each time Johnny caught her before she got to the city limits. He dragged her back and gave her what he called "consequences." These consequences resulted in black eyes, a broken tooth, a broken finger. It put Delores out of commission for a while, but Johnny considered the loss of income as a cost of doing business.

"The only way you get out of here," Johnny would say, "is if you die or I do."

Given that choice, it was no wonder that Johnny ended up on the wrong end of a stiletto.

The police report stated that two of Johnny's girls, Sugar (Maria Gomez) and Spice (Jane Chin) saw our client charging into Johnny's apartment with a look of anger and determination. After a few minutes, she came running out, blood on her hands, screaming. She ran down the railroad tracks toward the old switching yard and hid there for a night before the cops finally lured her out with hot coffee and donuts. She was cold, hungry, resigned. Her unfortunate statement when arrested for murder: "Somebody had to kill him."

Delores's wealthy family at first was going to let Delores suffer a Public Defender. But when the lawyer, an overworked man in his fifties, kept trying to get her to take a deal for Second Degree Murder—fifteen to life—they panicked and hired Minerva.

"First I talked to Sugar and Spice," I said.

"At the same time?" Minerva said, disapprovingly.

"They wouldn't talk to me any other way," I said. "They insisted on being interviewed together."

"Interesting," Minerva said. She stroked her chin and closed her eyes. "And what did those two young ladies tell you?"

"That Johnny ran a class outfit. His girls didn't walk the streets. Their gentlemen callers made appointments. He called it an escort service. Except he didn't let the girls off the apartment grounds."

"Which is how he kept track how many gentlemen each employee entertained and how much money changed hands," Minerva said thoughtfully.

I nodded.

"Sugar says she and her friend Spice were taking a well-deserved break in the courtyard of the apartment house. They were smoking, making jokes about the size of their customers'…uh…" I looked over at the child. Her crayons were still touching the book but they weren't moving.

Minerva put a hand up and I stopped.

"You observed the courtyard," she said.

I pulled out a diagram I had drawn. Minerva's gray eyes lit up.

"Outstanding," she said in the tone of a teacher encouraging a student who had just put two and two together successfully. She took a moment to examine the layout.

The courtyard was a long rectangle. The apartments were on either side, six in all. Four were used for business. The apartments were two story units with an upstairs for a large bedroom and a downstairs for kitchen and living room. Johnny lived in the apartment on the north end, along with two huge mastiff dogs and a Chihuahua. Like his chosen namesake, Johnny Hades chose to guard his domain with a three headed canine team.

His main girl, accountant, bill payer, office manager of sorts was Luz Gomez. She lived in the apartment directly opposite Johnny's. She was also his quasi-wife without benefit of clergy.

A walkway split the courtyard. I had notated on the diagram where Sugar and Spice smoked and gossiped when our client came running out of Johnny's apartment door.

"In the back is a parking lot. In the front of the apartment house, which faced the street, was where Sugar and Spice stood," I told the boss.

"Sugar said, 'We'd been out there no more'n five minutes when we saw Venus come out of the parking lot. Even from where I was at, I could see she was pissed off. She looked like she had her mind made up, like she was gonna do something.'" Of course, after a murder, witnesses often have a "memory" of the suspect looking determined to kill. For all we knew, Delores could have been suffering from a bout of gas.

"'And no one else went into Johnny's place,' Miss Spice told me. As if on cue."

Minerva smiled at me.

"You think they were told what to say?" she asked.

"It sounded well-rehearsed," I said.

"Proceed with the report of your interview," Minerva said. She stole a glance at Aphrodite, who abandoned all pretense of coloring.

"Sugar told me, 'Venus went into Johnny's place. It was real quiet. Quiet like it is before something bad happens. Then she comes out running and screaming.'

"'Screaming bloody murder,' Miss Spice added. 'She ran right past us, blood all over her hands. She doesn't even see us. She just runs out into the street.'"

Minerva leaned over and extracted a legal pad from her desk. She made a quick note, then nodded at me to proceed.

"I had my suspicions about those two doing a comedy routine of mostly fiction. But then I talked to a third person who saw Venus running."

Minerva cocked her head at the same moment her daughter did. The boss tapped the pen on the desk.

"Her next appointment, I presume," she said.

"Sugar's seven o'clock."

"And his name is…"

"Charlie Babbit. A reluctant witness, as you might guess. I promised him we wouldn't call him unless absolutely necessary. Which it's not because he pretty much confirmed what Sugar and Spice told me."

"Verbatim, please," Minerva said.

I read from my notebook.

"He said this: 'I was coming to see my good friend Miss Sugar. We were making small talk in the courtyard. She smoked a cigarette. Everything was calm. Then I heard a girl scream. Next thing I know this girl is running past us, yelling for Jesus.'"

"Jesus?" Minerva asked.

"That's what he said."

"What else did he observe?"

"That was it."

"Blood?" Minerva asked.

I checked my notes.

"He said nothing about blood."

Minerva nodded and made another note on the tablet. There were no signs of blood on the client when the cops arrested her. But the Deputy District Attorney handling the case insisted that Delores had plenty of time to clean herself in the hours it took to find her.

"He heard only the running woman screaming?" Minerva asked. I checked my notes.

"That's all he mentioned."

"Mother, the dogs," Aphrodite interjected. I looked over at the child. Her eyes regarded me intently, a look she had learned from her mother.

"Yes, love," the boss said. "I see what you mean."

"If you're thinking of that old Sherlock Holmes dodge about the curious incident of the dog barking—or not barking, as it were," I said, "forget it. Sugar and Spice tell me that our client got along well with the dogs. They knew her. They wouldn't have stirred when she came and went."

Minerva regarded me with the glint of disappointment on her face.

"Where did the dogs stay? Upstairs or down?"

"Wherever Johnny wanted them," I said. "The cops say that when they came to get the body the dogs were drowsing in the downstairs kitchen. They barked when the cops came in, but not so much that the police felt threatened."

Minerva nodded.

"What about this quasi-wife, Miss Gomez? What did she say?"

"She said she slept through most of it. She woke when she heard our client screaming bloody murder."

"Is that the term she used?" Minerva said. "'Bloody murder?'"

"The exact term," I said.

"Interesting," the boss said, making more notes. She turned to her child.

"What do you think, Aphrodite?"

"I want to know what happened to the dogs," the girl said seriously.

"An excellent question," her mother said encouragingly. I thought it was a foolish question. The dogs were not suspects. Still, to indulge the boss and her girl, I looked through the police report.

"Well, the two larger dogs, Sirius and Regus, they are still at the complex. I believe they are still in Johnny's apartment, as they evidently don't like Luz."

"That's important," the child said.

"Okay," I said doubtfully. "According to Sugar, Johnny thought it was funny that Luz was spooked by the dogs. He made her feed them every night about six. He evidently liked watching her shiver while trying to avoid getting devoured herself."

"A cruel-hearted man," Minerva said.

"It is telling," the child said.

"As for the little dog, the Chihuahua, he was named Cerberus," I said. "And he…uh…looks like he died of a heart attack the same day Johnny died. A weird coincidence."

Minerva and Aphrodite looked at one another knowingly.

"That's all I can tell you," I said.

Minerva sat back down in the visitor's chair.

"What is your next move, Mr. Robinson?"

"Not much I can do. I can talk to the other two girls who worked for Johnny to see if they have a different story, but my guess is that they don't. Seems like we've run into a brick wall on this one, boss."

Minerva nodded. Then she regarded her daughter.

"Aphrodite, what do you think Mr. Robinson should do next?"

"I think he needs to ask Luz whether the dogs all ate out of the same bowl."

I smiled indulgently. But the boss actually took this seriously.

"Yes, Mr. Robinson. I believe that should be your next task." She wrote something on her legal pad, then tore off the sheet and handed it to me. "Ask Luz this exact question, no variation. Oh, and bring Lt. Holden with you. And bring your revolver."

"That seems a bit extreme," I said.

"Nonetheless, it is my recommendation."

I was dismissed to pursue this useless errand.

* * * *

I called Lt. Holden even though I thought he would laugh at me when I explained what I was about to do. But he was quiet for a moment.

"Minerva told you to do this?" He said. "And she told you to bring me? And your gun?"

"Yes," I said apologetically. "I know it's crazy but—"

"But she's got a track record that can't be ignored. I'll meet you there in half an hour."

* * * *

Lt. Holden and I walked into the apartment complex of the late Johnny Hades. I could hear the dogs rousing at our footsteps, barking in a desultory manner from inside of the apartment. We happened to catch Luz as she was coming from feeding the dogs.

"Are you back?" she said to both of us.

"Just one question," I said. She was a thin dirt-blond woman with a weary face.

"One question, yet you brought the police," she said, gesturing at Lt. Holden. I merely nodded. I don't like telling witnesses that I have a question from Minerva. Her reputation for discerning the impossible makes folks clam up.

"Well, go ahead, then," she said wearily. "I have finances to go over and I need to talk to Spice about a complaint I got from one of her clients."

I opened the paper Minerva had given me and asked the question exactly:

"When you feed the dogs, do they all eat out of one bowl?"

Lt. Holden held a poker face, but I could see that he was trying to figure out what the hell Minerva had been thinking.

Luz looked at me in consternation.

"Is that all?" She said. "Did your boss write that out for you? The witch." She opened the door to Johnny's apartment and hissed one word:

"Attack."

The dogs roused themselves and began to bark fiercely. Both Lt. Holden and I didn't stop to wonder why. We ran like hell.

I could hear the heavy footpads of both mastiffs lumbering behind me. I had been a linebacker in my high school before going into the Army and kept in shape. But I knew I wasn't going to outrun the dogs.

Instead, I spun around to face them. The lead mastiff leapt at me and I hit him with a roundhouse kick. He flew against the side of the apartment with a surprised whine. The second dog stopped suddenly when he saw what happened to his mate. This gave me the chance to hit him in the jaw with a straight-ahead kick, which brought him down.

"You worthless sons of bitches," Luz screamed at the dogs. She reached into the back pocket of her jeans, but I already had my revolver pointed it at her heart.

"Easy or hard," I said. "Your choice."

She lay on the ground. Lt. Holden relieved her of a .22 pistol and put handcuffs on her.

"Some watchdogs they are," she muttered. The dogs were rousing themselves. They gave me wide berth and slunk back into Johnny's apartment.

"You got 'em good," Miss Spice said, emerging from another apartment. "I've been afraid of those monsters since I came here. Johnny used them to keep us in line. When he died, that bitch did the same thing. She made sure that Sugar and I would tell you the same thing. Now I know why." She walked up to me and kissed me on the cheek. "If you want to spend some time with me, no charge, you can come visit whenever you want."

I decided not to tell Minerva of the offer.

* * * *

I returned to the office before five o'clock.

"So, Mr. Robinson," Minerva said, "I am told by the police that your mission was successful." She stood by the statue of Lady Justice which she kept on a pedestal against the far wall. She looked over a volume of California Reports. Aphrodite still colored in her book at the enormous desk.

"Mission?" I asked.

"Surely you knew that I was sending you on something more than an inquiry," she said. Ah, Minerva. Ever the strategist, using me as her unwitting but willing pawn.

"I suppose I did," I said. "But I'm not sure what the hell happened, other than that I was chased by two very large dogs."

"Which Lt. Holden tells me you handled well with that peculiar fighting style you learned overseas," she said. "*Gung Fu*, isn't it?"

"That's the Chinese pronunciation, yes," I said. "Boss, could you please explain what happened so that I'm not up all night trying to figure it out for myself?"

Aphrodite had a small smile on her face as she carefully colored in in her book.

"Perhaps Aphrodite would like to explain it," the Boss said. Great, I thought. Now I'm going to be lectured to by a nine-year-old.

"It was the dogs," the child said. "In medieval times the king in the castle would have lots of big dogs to defend the castle and a few small dogs to wake the big dogs up. The small dogs were high strung and would hear things and start barking long before the big dogs knew what was happening. When I heard Johnny Hades had two big dogs and one small one, it sounded like this is what he was doing. Simple."

"Okay," I said. "I can see that. Johnny never knew if a rival would try to attack, so he kept watchdogs."

"Cerberus," Minerva said absently, "was the watchdog of Hades. Which is why he called the Chihuahua that name. The small dog was the trigger for the larger dogs."

"All well and good," I said. "But that doesn't explain why Luz went crazy when I asked her about the food bowl."

"Also simple," Aphrodite said, assuming the teaching tone she no doubt learned from the nuns. "The dogs should have barked the night Johnny Hades was killed."

"I thought that was explained by the fact that the dogs knew our client. And, for that matter, Luz. They wouldn't have barked at either woman entering to kill Johnny."

"But the evidence of three separate witnesses was that when Delores came out screaming, that's all they heard. No barking from the dogs. Even if the dogs knew her, they would have barked at her screaming. But they didn't."

"Which means?" I asked.

"They were drugged, of course," Minerva said impatiently.

Aphrodite nodded.

"They had to have been drugged. And how do you give a dog medicine? You put it in his food. And who fed the dogs? Luz. Why would Luz want to drug the dogs? So she could go up and kill Johnny without the dogs barking to alert everyone."

"Ah," I said.

"The fact that poor Cerberus died means that the dogs all ate out of the same bowl. Luz would have had to put a lot of the sleeping drugs in the food to put the big dogs asleep, but that same dose would have killed a small, high-strung dog." Aphrodite gave me a girlish smile. "Simple," she said.

"I see." I looked at the child's professorial expression. It was unnerving.

"So why did she kill her husband?"

"That matters little," Minerva said. "We have done our duty to the client by relieving her of a murder charge." She must've seen the dissatisfied look on my face. Aphrodite spoke up.

"She probably was tired of Johnny calling the shots and making the money," the child said. "And Mom's client was being difficult. This was a way to get rid of both problems. She told her girls to say our client had blood on her hands when she didn't. And Luz herself emphasized 'bloody murder' when no one else did. Simple."

I regarded Aphrodite for a moment, then gave her a solemn bow.

"I defer to the superior intellect in the room," I said. "And I will ever be your student, oh wise Aphrodite."

Mother and child regarded me with the same benevolent expression of a goddess.

✗

Mark Bruce is a disabled Vietnam-Era Veteran (Sgt. USAF, stationed in Italy and Turkey). A solo lawyer practicing divorce and criminal law in San Bernardino, Bruce now lives in Barstow, California. (Barstow is name-checked in "Get Your Kicks on Route 66.") He won the 2018 Black Orchid Novella Award for his story "Minerva James and the Goddess of Justice." More Minerva stories have been published in *Alfred Hitchcock's Mystery Magazine* and other publications. His son Adam is getting a PhD in Aerospace Engineering at Michigan University—that's right, his son is a rocket scientist. At present Mr. Bruce lives with Mariah, a stuffed mermaid, and his writing-support dragon Ferdinand.

A WALK IN THE PARK

LIS ANGUS

Dooley trotted to the top of the hill, tail high, nose raised. A breeze ruffled his thick fur, and tall trees sighed overhead. He sniffed. Gopher scent, old. Porcupine, more recent. Tree and plant smells, unimportant. Mice, here now, in the underbrush near the path; he could hear them rustling. He cocked his head but didn't feel drawn to pursue them.

He could hear Boss close behind him on the path, and his attention shifted to her. Her stride was strong and steady. Her scent reached out to him, familiar as his own.

"Hey, Dooley," she said, coming up beside him. She knelt down and wrapped her arms around him, stroking his fur, rubbing his ears. He arched his neck to greet her caress. "Good boy, Dooley. Great fall morning, isn't it?" He gave her a quick lick on the face. She moved her head away, laughing.

They were a team. She was a good Boss, and his loyalty to her was unquestioning. She had been his Boss for a long time now. He had only a dim memory of his other boss, the man who had trained him.

He trotted ahead again, Boss moving quickly behind him. He listened for her footsteps, setting his pace to match hers. They walked here almost every morning, following one of the several trails that wound through woods and parkland and along the lakefront. They walked early, just after sunrise. Sometimes they passed other people, walking or running, with or without dogs. He knew each one's scent.

As they left the trees and moved into the open grass between woods and the rocky shoreline, he saw two people up ahead, a man and a woman. They weren't on the path but seemed to be coming from the rocks by the water. He had seen these two here in the park before, though never previously off the path. Both were thin and dark, and not young. The woman moved as if she were sick, and always walked a few steps behind the man, struggling to keep up. The man never turned to look or speak to her.

Dooley focused his ears on them; he could hear the woman wheezing, but neither person spoke. As they reached the pathway, the wind brought their scent in a strong gust. Dooley's nostrils twitched. He recognized their scents: each had an individual person-odor, overlaid by something he recognized as a food-smell, though not one he was familiar with.

The woman also always smelled afraid. She was afraid of the man. Sometimes the fear smell was stronger, sometimes weaker. Today it was strong.

The man walked in the center of the path, not moving to the side to pass as most people did. He looked straight ahead, not glancing at either Boss or Dooley. The woman hurried after him.

Boss moved onto the grass to let them by. As they passed, Dooley got a strong whiff of another scent, one he hadn't smelled on them before. One that sliced through to old, terrible memories and made his hackles rise.

He stopped and turned, watching them, a low growl rumbling in this throat.

"Dooley!" Boss hurried up and grasped his collar. "Hey, boy, what's the problem?"

He growled again and moved to follow them, but Boss held him back. She spoke soothingly and he settled back on his haunches, still rumbling but obedient to the restraint. The scent faded as the couple reached the trees.

He turned again and looked up at Boss. She patted his shoulder and said, "Let's go, boy." He trotted beside her as they resumed their walk. They reached the point where the man and woman had joined the path. He could hear the waves crashing on the rocks at the shoreline, just below.

Now he could smell that odor again. It was stronger here. He bounded ahead, off the path and down the rocks, following the ever-more-pungent smell.

It smelled of meat, spoiled meat.

It unlocked memories of smoke, people screaming and shouting, children crying. Explosive noises, men attacking the village. His old boss coming out of a collapsed building, a small girl lying limp in his arms, a bloody cloth wrapped around the stump of her leg. Memories of a later time when his boss, and many other people, lay on the ground, still and unmoving, the spoiled-meat smell filling the air. And despite everything Dooley tried, his boss did not get up again.

He could smell that odor again now. It was coming from the rocks ahead. Something between them, wedged in tight. Smooth and dark, like the bags Boss put garbage in and took out to the street. He grabbed a corner and pulled, hard, yanking the bag up and out from between the rocks. He dragged it over to where Boss was standing.

"Dooley, what do you have there? What did you find?" Boss bent to open the bag. "Whew, it stinks." She waved her hand in front of her face.

Then she screamed.

* * * *

The television was on. A young woman was speaking. "And in a shocking development earlier today, police have retrieved what they believe to be the dismembered limbs of an elderly person. We go to Jed McQuire for more."

The TV image shifted to show a young man standing outdoors, his hair mussed by the wind. He lifted his microphone. "Earlier today, a woman walking her dog here in Waterfront Park made a gruesome discovery. Her dog found a green plastic garbage bag, apparently hidden in the rocks by the water. When she opened it, it contained a severed hand and forearm. She immediately called the police, who in a preliminary search found another hand and a thigh, also in plastic bags. Police say the limbs appear to be those of an adult, probably an elderly woman. The investigation is ongoing. Police are looking for a middle-aged couple, a man and a woman, who were seen in the area this morning. And now back to you, Pamela."

* * * *

Dooley lay on the floor, watching Boss. A man wearing a uniform sat on the sofa.

"You know, I don't think I can be much help," she said. "I've passed both of them walking in the park before—they seem to like to walk early in the morning, around the same time as I often go—but to be honest I've always paid more attention to her appearance than to his. She always looks cowed and frightened. I felt sorry for her, always scurrying along after him. In fact, I was concerned about her: a few weeks ago, she seemed to have a black eye, though she had a scarf covering part of her face, so it was hard to tell. I worried that she was being abused. I looked at him too, especially then, but I'm afraid I don't remember enough specific details about his appearance to be of help. I don't know if I'd even recognize him again, if he were alone. I just recognized them as a couple."

The man in the uniform cleared his throat. "Well, that's possible, ma'am, but we'd appreciate it if you could spend some time with the artist anyway. Even an approximate likeness will give us something to go on."

* * * *

The television was on again. "Pamela Jones here with the six o'clock news. Just before news time, there was a breaking development linking two unsolved murder cases here in the city. To tell us about it, we go to Jed McQuire."

The young man stood in front of a small apartment building, snow swirling in his hair. "Viewers will remember Maria Nagy, whose strangled body was found in November in the apartment where she had been living with her husband, Peter Nagy, and her elderly mother. Neighbors interviewed after the murder said that Mr. and Mrs. Nagy moved to Canada from Hungary a year ago, with her mother joining them about six months later. When Maria Nagy's body was found, neither her mother nor her husband could be located. Police announced this afternoon that, according to DNA evidence, the severed limbs found in garbage bags at Waterfront Park in October belonged to Maria Nagy's mother. It's now clear that the mother, whose name isn't yet known, was killed about a month before her daughter. The rest of the mother's body has not been found. Neighbors say the family was very reclusive, though they at times heard raised voices from inside the apartment. Police are stepping up their search for Peter Nagy, who is now a suspect in both deaths."

* * * *

Dooley trotted along, breathing in the crisp air. A sudden thaw had opened the snowbound paths, and Boss had driven them both to the park for a vigorous walk through the woods and down past the shore. "We can't let that experience spoil the best walking route in the city," she said. "And it'll be good to get outside for a real workout in the fresh air again, now that spring's almost here."

He could hear birds twittering in the trees, and could hear rivulets running under the snow still lying beneath the underbrush. He could tell that a jackrabbit had passed by sometime recently, but otherwise there were no small animals about yet.

Boss was close behind him and keeping pace. She was whistling. They left the woods and moved toward the rocky shore. Dooley was alert. He could sense that Boss was especially anxious about this part of the route, where they had found the plastic bags with the spoiled-meat smell.

As they neared the shore, Dooley noticed movement ahead—there was someone behind a tree, a short distance from the path.

At the same time, he smelled a distinctive odor: the scent of the man they had seen here before with the woman. With the odor came the man—darting out from behind the tree, moving quickly, running toward Boss. He held his arm high, with something long and sharp in his hand.

Though the man didn't have that spoiled-meat smell on him today, the memory of the smell was suddenly sharp in Dooley's mind. He didn't hesitate. He leapt to intercept the man, clamping his teeth into the man's upraised wrist. The man shrieked and hit at Dooley's head with his other hand. Dooley's momentum carried them both forward, onto the rocks. They both fell over, Dooley's teeth in an iron grip around the man's wrist.

Dooley heard footsteps on the rocks behind him. He felt something move past his ear and heard a heavy thump. Suddenly the man jerked and went limp.

Dooley's teeth were still clamped to his wrist when the men with the uniforms came to talk to Boss and take the man's body away.

* * * *

The man in the uniform sat on Boss' sofa again. "He's definitely Peter Nagy," he said. "He may have followed you to the park, though it's possible that he was there already, clambering around on the rocks. Who knows what significance that location had for him—it's where he tried to hide his mother-in-law's body. In any case, he must have recognized you. He probably thought you could identify him, and here was his chance. That's a lethal knife he was carrying; you're lucky your dog was so quick to react. And, to be frank, I'm not sorry the guy hit his head on a rock when he fell. His death was an accident, but sometimes I think there's something called natural justice."

Boss sipped her drink; ice clinked in the glass. "Well, it's over now. I'm just glad Dooley was with me and was so alert."

"Tell me: was he trained as a defense dog?"

"I'm not sure what training he's had. My brother is in the Armed Forces and was stationed in Afghanistan. He found Dooley in a village that had been attacked by insurgents; Dooley seemed to have belonged to one of the people who had been killed. My brother took pity on him and brought him back to Canada, but he couldn't keep a dog on the base, so he gave Dooley to me. And it's worked out fine: he's a wonderful dog."

Boss leaned over and stroked Dooley's fur. Dooley leaned his nose on his paws and closed his eyes.

This time he hadn't failed his Boss.

Lis Angus is a Canadian suspense writer. Early in her career she worked with children and families in crisis, and later as a policy advisor, business writer and editor. Her novel, *Not Your Child*, was a finalist in the 2021 Daphne du Maurier Mystery/Suspense awards, and is being published by Wild Rose Press. Lis now lives south of Ottawa with her husband. You can visit her website at www.lisangus.com.

MUDBOUND
VERONICA LEIGH

August 1932
Ouabache, Indiana

Sheriff Claire Williams eased her foot on the brake, stopping the Model A Ford a hundred feet from the crime scene. She turned off the car and looked over the dashboard once more to ensure she hadn't forgotten anything. Still unaccustomed to driving, she couldn't afford any mistakes. *Not now.* Opening the driver's door, she climbed out, shut it and made her way to the small group crowded around the deceased. Her husband's boots weighed down her feet, but she didn't have any sturdy footwear of her own that she could wear while clumping about the muddied countryside.

Claire pushed her way past the crowd and disregarded the perturbed mumbles under the men's breath. Tilting her head to the side, she studied the unusual sight.

Warren Bartholomew was dead, buried waist deep in solidified mud and red as an overripe tomato on the verge of spilling out its innards. He'd been a swarthy man, filthy and loud, and the general consensus of the tiny town of Ouabache was that Warren was a waste of perfectly good skin. A drunkard, he frequented all the illegal local stills, visited prostitutes, started brawls, never paid his debts, and mistreated his family.

Claire pursed her lips. *No one's going to mourn this man.*

"Mrs. Williams—" Deputy Frank greeted her, a pencil and pad of paper in hand.

"Sheriff Williams, if you please," Claire corrected gently as she could. The last thing she wanted was to ruffle anyone's feathers, but she did want acknowledgement for her inherited position.

"Right." Deputy Frank grunted, and she could hear the short, thin man grumble to himself.

Her cheeks flushed. She was well aware that there were others in Vigo County who could perform the job of sheriff better than she, but the badge was pinned to the bodice of her dress, above her breast. Her husband, Reginald, had been elected sheriff and had held the position for three months until he was killed during investigation of an illegal still. Reginald wasn't cold in the grave before the commissioner approached her and swore her in. "Widow's Succession," was what the commissioner called it. Too numb with grief to protest, Claire complied with his wishes and accepted the post. After all, times were hard and she needed a way to support herself, but she had never worked outside of the home. She and

Reginald had married when he returned home from the Great War and she settled right into housekeeping.

Who else knew Reginald's plans and what he intended better than me? she pondered. From the time he was young, her husband had wanted to make a difference in the world. Now was her chance to fulfill his dreams.

Deputy Frank cleared his throat and spat a wad of phlegm off to the side. "Well, never have seen such a thing."

"Me either. Lord have mercy." Claire silently said a prayer for the man's wretched soul. "I can't say I'm surprised, though I always figured Mr. Bartholomew would die by pickling his liver."

"No one's gonna miss him, that's for sure. May not be Christian to say, but could be a blessing in disguise for the family. Such a strange accident and a strange way to go."

Claire nodded. *It is a strange way to go.* For months, the valley hadn't received a drop of rain. According to the newspapers and radio, the rest of the country was also suffering from drought. Then, without warning, for two weeks it rained. And rained, and rained, and rained. Not that it helped the heat; in fact, it made it worse, and a choking humidity descended upon the valley. The unpaved roads of Ouabache and the countryside turned to brown slop. When the rain stopped, the ground solidified once more. Sometime between then and now, Warren Bartholomew was sucked waist-deep into the mud. He died, with the sun baking him to death. Far out in the countryside, no one would have heard his screams, and if a hobo hadn't been traveling through the woods and reported the sight to the deputy, only God knows how long Warren would have been there.

Out of habit, Claire went to brush her hair behind her right ear, but it was not there. Her dark hair was drawn back into a severe tail and clasped together to keep from hanging down in her face. Before shrugging off Bartholomew's death as a freak accident, she closely studied the scene.

Then she saw something.

Claire carefully approached and, squinting, her suspicion was confirmed. There was a gash on the crown of Warren's head. Due to his dark hair and sunburnt scalp, it had gone unnoticed.

"No, no accident. Someone hit him. There's a gash here." Claire pointed her finger toward the wound.

Deputy Frank crouched and made a scoffing sound, but Claire didn't care. She knew she was right. And if Reginald were here, he wouldn't let it go.

Someone had hit Warren Bartholomew in the head.

Warren Bartholomew had been murdered.

"Photograph him, take notes with thorough description, and excavate him. Have the coroner examine him," Claire ordered, noting how Deputy Frank bristled under her instructions. The deputy had assumed—as had many others, herself included—that he would be sheriff after Reginald's death. The commissioner had other ideas. Reginald never completely trusted Deputy Frank, but he had never said why. Claire figured she would have to make her own judgments, though she did find it hard to respect a man who openly resented her.

Claire backed away from the body and was about to return to her car when she stopped short. She noticed a small cleft in the dirt off to the side of the road. It wasn't natural. "There looks to be a mark here." She knelt down and traced the outer edge of it, never touching it. "Appears to be from the heel of a boot. Take a plaster of it."

"It might have been one of ours." Deputy Frank suggested, making no attempt to hide his skepticism.

Claire glanced at the four pairs of muddied boots. It could have been one of theirs. But their boots were bigger and, from their weight, they would have made a larger and deeper impression. This mark was small and not shaped like a man's boot.

"As I said, take a plaster of it. I think the killer stood here," she replied. Before Deputy Frank could argue any further, she returned to her Model A.

* * * *

It didn't take long for Claire to reach the Bartholomew farm, five miles from where Warren Bartholomew died. She shut off the car and left it in the middle of the road, unafraid of anyone coming along to disturb it. The Bartholomews' ramshackle house sat on a knoll, smack dab in the middle of nowhere, with the woods and the Wabash River as their nearest neighbors. By living close to the mosquito-infested river, the Bartholomews' health was in peril. The thick swarming insects carried malaria and one bite could strike a healthy man down in the prime of his life.

Claire followed the small path up to the porch, nodding to two women who emerged from the house. She could make out a handful of children working in the fields and, though she had seen the Bartholomew family in church, she couldn't recall who was who. This was part of the job she wished she could avoid, yet there was no way around it.

Rose Bartholomew moved closer and warmly greeted Claire. "Mrs.— Sheriff—Williams!" The woman reddened over her mistake and smoothed the wrinkles from her threadbare frock. Her greasy hair was drawn back in a braid and hung limply over one shoulder. Dark bits of dirt settled into the wrinkles around her eyes and mouth. But what caught Claire's attention was the woman's cracked and swollen lower lip. "Why are you here? Where's Warren?"

Claire sighed wearily. She hated to further crush this woman's already broken spirit, but she thought it best to be straightforward. "Mrs. Bartholomew, pardon me, I don't know how to tell you." She reached for Rose's dirt-encrusted hand and gave it a comforting squeeze. "But your husband is dead."

"Oh, good Lord!" the other woman exclaimed.

Claire glanced at her and felt foolish for having forgotten she was there. *Not very observant for a sheriff.* She would have to work on her observational skills and learn to commit facts to memory. Unlike the deputy, she could not afford to make a mistake.

Claire looked back at Rose, who had visibly blanched and then became unsteady. The other woman dragged over a rocking chair and guided Rose into it. "I—how?" Her eyes went glassy. "Was it a bad batch of gin?"

"No ma'am. Mr. Bartholomew appears to have had an accident." As Claire told the story, she watched Rose carefully, garnering her reactions. She felt safe crossing Rose off her list of suspects. She was a thin, mousy creature who had been beaten down by her husband and by life, and Claire doubted she had it in her to kill him. Even so, she had to make sure every "t" was crossed and every "i" was dotted. Reginald would do as much if he were running this investigation. "He was discovered on a dirt road. The road had softened from the rain and he seemed to have sunk down in there waist deep. When was the last time you saw him?"

"Y-yesterday at d-dawn." Rose poked around in her apron pockets for something and came away with nothing. The other woman drew a handkerchief from the pocket of her bibbed overalls and handed it to Rose. "He had planting to do and said he'd be in for dinner, but he never showed."

"Why didn't you send for me?" Claire asked.

"It's not uncommon for Warren to go to Terre Haute in the afternoons. Or be gone for days."

"What business did he have in Terre Haute?" Claire waited for Rose to respond to her question and found it odd when she didn't.

It was no secret that Warren Bartholomew was a frequent customer of the illegal stills in the area. Or that he was quarrelsome, loud, and clearly a brute to his wife and—in all likelihood—his family. Everyone turned a blind eye though. The world and the church offered no sanctuary to women and children living in sad situations. Rose and her family had no way out.

Once married, always married. Claire's heart clenched and she felt thankful that though her own husband died young, he was a good man and he loved her dearly.

"He whored around." The other woman harrumphed and gently patted Rose's shoulder. "He liked to go calling on Madam Brown's girls, and he left Rose and his children to do all of his work. Bastard. Well, I for one, am glad he's dead."

"And you are?" Claire arched one of her brows and looked the other woman up and down. She didn't know what to make of her.

"Marty Jennings." Marty promptly stuck her hand out and shook Claire's with three big pumps. Clad in bibbed overalls and a flannel shirt, Marty wore her hair cropped short, and she was as muscular as a man. "I'm Rose's sister."

Claire withdrew her hand from Marty's and flexed her fingers, relaxing them from the woman's tight grip. "Ladies, I am concerned. There is evidence of physical assault."

She continued to note their responses, determined not to miss anything. Rose's eyes watered and she shuddered, while Marty smirked and looked satisfied. It occurred to her that sisters couldn't have been more opposite than these two.

"Ah, so someone did him in." Marty snickered.

"Should I suspect you, Miss Jennings?" Claire asked.

"No." Marty shook her head. "I regret to say I didn't do it. I was with mother the whole day. She's an invalid."

Claire found this admission disappointing. Marty would have been the best candidate for Warren's murderer. She clearly hated the man for what he had done to her sister and seemed happy he was dead. From her muscled biceps, Marty would have been strong enough to kill a man, but something seemed off about her as a suspect.

"Mrs. Bartholomew," Claire felt a pinch on her bare forearm, glanced down, and found a mosquito biting her. She killed it, wrinkling her nose at the blood smear it left behind. "Where were you?"

"Here." Rose jutted her thumb in the direction of the front door. "I took dinner out to the children."

"Did your husband have any enemies?" A question with an obvious answer, considering how troublesome Warren Bartholomew was, but it had to be asked.

"Sheriff Williams, my husband wasn't well liked." Rose dabbed her eyes with the handkerchief Marty had given her and then hugged herself. "I wouldn't know where to begin. He had debts, he got into brawls, he stole, and he visited Madam Brown's girls. He would drink anything that made his cheeks gin blossom."

"We all wanted to kill him, but only one person was lucky enough," Marty said.

"All right. I'll be back later on when I know more." Claire started to turn around but stopped and, though it might not be considered professional or what Reginald would have done, she felt sorry for Rose Bartholomew. "I do apologize for being the bearer of bad tidings. Your whole family will be in my prayers, Mrs. Bartholomew."

Rose smiled and nodded her head appreciatively.

Claire left, feeling as perplexed as when she had arrived.

* * * *

Claire shivered and it wasn't because she was cold. No one could be cold in the middle of August in the Wabash Valley. A layer of suffocating perspiration clung to her like a second skin. Her burgundy frock made it worse, drawing the heat to her. The building's windows were wide open, but the air was stagnant and there was no breeze.

The naked corpse of Warren Bartholomew was laid out before her, on an old table in the rear examination room of the doctor's office. A sheet had been pulled up to the deceased's doubled chin and hid everything, and even though he was dead as a doornail, she remained unnerved by the wretched man. He seemed to bother her more now than when he was stuck in the ground.

Dead bodies bothered her. Death always had. Bodies, funerals, graveside services, grief—she did her utmost to avoid it. *I have to overcome this*, Claire reminded herself. As the sheriff of Ouabache, she and death would occasionally cross paths.

Jed Loving, the doctor and acting coroner, entered the room wearing a dingy apron and nodded to her respectfully. "Sheriff." The grizzled man shuffled up to the table and gave a hard sniff. "Warren Bartholomew's death seems well overdue."

Claire envied people like Jed Loving. Not much in the world appeared to faze the old man. A tall, lanky, wrinkled creature, the only hair he had was white and shrouded his cheeks and chin. His left cheek always bulged, from a wad of tobacco. He never spat in her presence, though. Or any other lady's.

"Well?" Claire willed herself to move closer to Warren.

"I gave him a thorough examination." Jed undid the ties and shed his blood-soiled apron, rolling it into a ball. He scrunched up his long nose. "He was in bad shape. It's a wonder he didn't keel over years ago. Pickled liver, blackened lungs, fat, dirty—"

"But how did he die?"

"Oh, it was the blow to his head, that's for sure." Jed clucked his tongue at the deceased. "That's what did him in. A hard object—a rock or a brick."

Claire's shoulders fell. While she had been convinced someone had killed Warren, part of her hoped she was mistaken and that Warren was the cause of his own demise. Now, with a murderer on the loose, it was her responsibility to find him. She couldn't count on her deputy to be of use. He didn't respect her. When she had asked Deputy Frank to question Ouabache's locals to see if they could shed light on Warren, he grumbled his complaints and stalked off. He never did report what he learned.

This case would be easier if the victim hadn't been universally despised. Either someone had led him down that path, knowing he would become mud-bound, or he fell in. Whoever was with him at the time, or later happened upon him, hit him.

"He had one foot in the grave before he was hit," Jed insisted. "Mr. Bartholomew had been out there in that mud awhile. Maybe three days before he died."

"Three days!" Claire repeated, astonished by this new bit of information.

"He was dehydrated and malnourished, sunburnt all over." Jed gestured to Warren's cracked lips, unaware of her epiphany. "Had sunburn on the insides of his cheeks."

Claire went to the nearest window and stood next to it, cursing herself for not bringing her purse. A church fan was in it, and she needed a little reprieve from the heat to organize her thoughts.

Rose and Marty lied to me. She wasn't naïve; people lied all the time. What she found perplexing was why the two women had misled her. Rose may have had a motive, but it wasn't in her nature to kill. Marty could have done it, but Claire felt in her heart of hearts that Marty hadn't killed him either. Not that she could prove their innocence; she was relying on instinct alone. However, they withheld pertinent information, a clear obstruction of justice.

"Mrs. Bartholomew and her sister said he had only been missing a day." Claire rubbed her brow, feeling a headache coming on, one triggered by the heat and by tension.

"Sister?" Jed turned around and faced her, flashing a befuddled expression. "Mrs. Bartholomew doesn't have a sister. I've known her family for years and she was an only child." He jutted his thumb towards Warren. "No, he was out there for more than a day. I'd bet my reputation on it."

Claire covered her mouth. Not only had Rose and Marty told her a falsehood about the length of time Warren had been missing, they had deceived her about the nature of their relationship. *Why claim to be sisters if they are simply close friends?* It didn't make any sense. The first lie about Warren had clearly been to throw her off about his time of death. She still didn't think either were guilty of murder, but they knew more than they had let on. But why lie about a friendship?

Unless they are more than friends.

The thought had come to her unbidden and she was about to dismiss it entirely. But it made sense. There was a closeness between Rose and Marty. It would be the perfect motive, to do away with a violent and unwanted husband. If they were discreet, they would be free to be together. But something told her that wasn't it. There was a big piece of the puzzle still missing. Rose and Marty might not have killed Warren, but she had a feeling they knew who did.

Claire extended her hand to Jed Loving and shook his. "Thank you for your time." She managed a strained smile.

The previous few days had left her spent, but Claire thought if she could talk with Rose and Marty again and confront them about their deceit, then she might actually be able to solve this case. Or a small part of it.

* * * *

Claire knocked forcefully on the front door of the Bartholomew home, impatient to speak to Rose and Marty again. When the door jerked open, she wasn't surprised to find Marty on the other side. The woman towered over her, but Claire squared her shoulders and refused to be intimidated.

"May I come in?" Claire brushed past Marty before the woman could respond.

She attempted to school her features to disguise her revulsion, but she feared she failed. The house repulsed her in every way imaginable. The putrid stench of rotted food, stale smoke, and unwashed bodies burned in her nostrils. Surveying the simple, shotgun house, she could tell that Rose had made attempts to clean. Everything was in its place and there was no clutter. The walls bore black smudges from pipe smoke and the floor was spotted by tobacco juice. There were no photographs or homemade art adorning the walls. Furniture was sparse and worn. No toys in sight for the children. Unlike many families, including the poorest of the poor, there was no radio.

This was Warren Bartholomew's doing. Claire furiously gritted her teeth. She had no connection to the deceased, yet he offended her. Warren spent his life causing misery wherever he went and wouldn't allow his family the simple comforts of what a home should have. He didn't want his wife and children to have anything but him. *No one should have to live like this.*

Rose crept over, wringing her chapped hands. "I'm glad you're here, sheriff. I want to confess." Her head drooped, reminding Claire of a whipped pup desperate for a corner to cower in. The woman's lip had healed some, but the effects of her husband's abuse would be present for a long while.

"Confess what? That Mr. Bartholomew was absent for longer than a day?" Claire pinned Rose with her unwavering gaze, unwilling to relent even though she felt guilty when the woman cringed. "Or confess that you two aren't related?"

"Confess that I killed my husband." Rose broke down into a sob, her shoulders shaking.

Marty rushed to Rose's side and brought her arm around her friend. "Don't believe her! I killed that bastard," the woman insisted, her raised voice echoing throughout the empty house. "You know it, sheriff. Rose couldn't harm a fly."

"Now, I do believe you on that score." Claire clasped her hands behind her back and paced. "What confuses me is why you misled me the other day and why you suddenly want to confess. Who are you really, Miss Jennings?"

Marty mashed her lips together, refusing to speak.

Rose claimed Marty's hand and reverently cradled it within her own. "Marty is my friend. My dearest friend." Her gentle voice cracked on the last word.

It was on the tip of Claire's tongue to ask if they were lovers, but she choose not to. She didn't think their relationship had anything to do with Warren's death. Another sheriff, even her husband, could make a case that Rose and Marty conspired to kill Warren to get him out of the way. She felt it wasn't her place to judge them, but if this became public, the remainder of Ouabache would. The same society that turned a blind eye to Warren's depravity, would condemn Rose and Marty. She would do her utmost to keep this discovery private.

It can't be a sin to love another person. Claire decided and believed that with every fiber of her being.

"I do believe you have it in you to kill a man, Miss Jennings, but I don't think you killed Warren." Claire paused in front of them, her hands still behind her back. Her gaze flickered back and forth between Rose and Marty. "There is so much about Warren's death that doesn't make sense. So much of the story has been left untold. I believe you two are protecting someone else."

She was surprised when Marty—not Rose—made a large gulping sound, betraying herself. Neither woman spoke up and Claire began to rack her brain, frantic to make these ladies tell the truth. Reginald never told her how he interrogated suspects.

"They're protecting me." An unfamiliar youthful voice piped up from behind.

Claire turned to find a young, boyish girl standing in the doorway. A smaller version of Rose, her blond hair was cropped short, and she was in bibbed overalls like Marty. A constellation of freckles dusted her nose and the apples of her cheeks. From her features and height, Claire estimated her to be around twelve.

"Hush, Kit!" Rose scolded and pointed in the opposite direction. "And go back outside."

Claire took a step closer to the girl, disregarding Marty's menacing expression. "Kit?"

"Short for Katherine." Kit nodded and her eyes rounded in fear. "I did it, I killed my pa."

"Stop it!" Marty broke away from Rose and wedged herself between Kit and Claire. "Sheriff, she is just a child. Now, I'm right here, a grown woman telling you I killed Warren Bartholomew. I—"

Claire dismissed the woman with a wave of her hand and was amazed that Marty actually obeyed. "Let the girl speak." She tilted her head to the side and sent Kit a warm, compassionate look. She glanced down at Kit's feet, and gestured to the girl's mud-caked boots. "I found a print from the heel of your boot at the scene."

"Yes, ma'am." Kit shuffled her feet. Bits of dirt flaked off. "Me and Pa were walking along that path near the woods and he stepped on a muddy patch and it sucked him in to his middle. He couldn't get out and I left him there."

Claire's heart palpitated painfully, disturbed by the girl's cavalier explanation. "Why would you do that, Kit?"

"'Cause I hated him and I wanted him to die." Kit replied without batting an eyelash. She crossed her arms defiantly. "He beat on us, you know? Ma, me, the younger ones, the animals. He liked to hurt people; I could tell by the look he'd get when he did it. He made Ma cry all the time. The night before he fell into that muddy patch, he knocked a plate to the floor and made Ma lap it up like a dog. Pa hit my little brother with a bootjack." The girl paused, hesitating before she continued her story. "Lately he's been looking at me…wrongly."

Claire heard Rose release a pathetic gasp, but she refused to tear her gaze away from the girl. Such things were rarely discussed in polite company, but Claire had a sinking suspicion that Warren's depravity extended farther than physical and verbal abuse.

"What does 'wrongly' mean?" Claire asked.

Kit lowered her head and studied her dirty boots. "He walked in on me bathing last Sunday and didn't leave 'til I was done." She sniffed but didn't cry. "Pa brought me to the woods for a reason."

Claire bit down on her tongue to maintain her silence. For two cents, she would have killed Warren Bartholomew herself. Anyone worth their salt would have done as much. It was a mystery to her why someone else hadn't done away with him years ago.

"So, when he dropped into that mud, I decided to leave him there." Kit resumed her tale, still dry-eyed. Her expression relayed the emptiness within her. Her pa drained the life out of her. "Ma would think he ran off and then maybe she'd move us somewhere else. I figured an animal would get him, but none of them did. I went back several times, he was still alive."

"And?" Claire reached over and gently squeezed Kit's bony shoulder, offering the poor girl some much-needed sympathy. "I know that isn't all that happened, Kit. Finish your story, please."

Kit solemnly nodded. "The last time I saw him, Pa was cussing up a blue streak, saying he'd kill me when he got out. I didn't want to die and I didn't want to be looked at wrongly or get beat on anymore. I took a big rock and hit him. He went quiet then. I threw the rock in the blue hole." The girl gulped and the rims of her eyes reddened, but still the tears didn't fall. "I killed my Pa and I'd do it again if I had a chance."

"Lord have mercy," Claire whispered, praying that the Lord would.

The single piece of evidence rested at the bottom of the blue hole, a lake too deep for divers to reach the bottom.

Rose went to her daughter's side and wrapped her arm around the girl. "Please, don't arrest her. This is my fault. I should have taken the children and run off ages ago." She held out both of her wrists for them to be cuffed. "Take me instead."

Claire's face grew warm. She didn't have a set of handcuffs with her, which was embarrassing. "Mrs. Bartholomew, did you suspect that Kit killed her father?"

Marty took her place on the other side of Kit. "Rose didn't, but I did. We noticed Kit kept wandering off. I followed Kit the last time she went to check on her pa and I saw her strike him. We wanted to protect her. We didn't think you could tell how long he had been in the ground." For the first time since their introduction, Marty looked vulnerable. "Please, Sheriff, the girl was put in a horrible predicament with no way out. I watched her kill him and I regret that I didn't do it myself a long time ago." She pressed her palm to her chest. "So, please, let the blame fall on me."

Claire observed the three and shook her head miserably. She found herself begging the Lord for guidance, because she wanted to do the right thing. Unfortunately, she didn't know what that was.

What would Reginald do? Gooseflesh prickled her skin as she finally understood that Reginald had nothing to do with this. Reginald was dead; he was no longer sheriff. She was. Ouabache was her responsibility and fulfilling the duties of sheriff could not be about her husband. This was her chance to find her place in this world. A place outside of the home.

Lord, please, give me wisdom. To arrest and imprison a young girl seemed wrong. Kit Bartholomew had been driven to killing her pa and she clearly feared for her life if Warren did manage to crawl out of the mud.

Society failed Kit and the Bartholomew family. The church looked the other way.

As far as I'm concerned, it was self-defense, Claire decided, but she knew it might not be that simple in the court of law. There was no telling how a jury might judge Kit. It was a good thing she had not brought Deputy Frank along, otherwise he would have immediately arrested Kit.

There was only one thing she could do and it would be done with a clear conscience.

Cover it up. Reginald might have arrested Kit, but she would not.

Claire laced her fingers together and cast a sympathetic glance at the three. "I think—I think it's a shame Warren Bartholomew died the way he did. A real shame. Falling and hitting his head and then stumbling into the muddy patch. His senses must have been dulled by alcohol." She locked eyes with Marty, who would likely assume the position as head of this family, and nodded to her. "A freak accident, is what it was. You can't prevent this sort of thing."

Rose's hand flew to her mouth to stifle a gasp.

Kit's face crumbled and she finally broke down sobbing.

Claire coughed, feeling a lump forming in her own throat. "Well, I won't take up any more of your time. Let me know if there is anything more I can do for you. You will be in my prayers."

She departed the Bartholomew property and didn't dare look back.

* * * *

Claire shifted uncomfortably in her chair at the desk in the sheriff's office. She had been sitting there for hours and her backside was growing numb. Once more she reviewed the paperwork, feeling confident that the report she had written sounded plausible. She wrote in a firm, clear hand exactly what she promised the Bartholomews she would say. It was wrong, she was covering up a crime.

It's for the greater good, Claire reasoned, leaning back in her seat. Otherwise, a girl would be imprisoned. Rose and Marty shouldn't have to pay for a crime they didn't commit. She would pray for forgiveness, ask God to understand, and try to do better in the future.

She arranged the papers in a neat little stack and, clearing her throat, she signaled to the deputy who was whittling. "Would you file this?"

Deputy Frank stood and brushed the wood shavings from his trousers, knocking them to the floor. He gave no thought to the mess he made. He snatched the papers from her and moseyed to the filing cabinet, quickly reading her account before putting it away. "How the hell…pardon me, Sheriff Williams." He spun around, his mouth slack. "How on God's green earth could the coroner declare Warren Bartholomew's death an accident? The blow to the head, that heel print? It doesn't make a lick of sense."

"Because it was an accident," Claire answered, drawing in a deep breath. She had to convince the deputy. If she didn't convince him, there would be no chance of convincing anyone else. "After a thorough investigation, I realized it was an accident."

"Really? But what about the coroner?" Deputy Frank reminded her.

After discreet conversation with Jed Loving about what happened and the situation Kit Bartholomew was in, he had agreed to change the cause of death. She trusted he would not mention it again. As for the deputy, she intentionally chose not to confide the truth to him. Her husband's doubts about Deputy Frank continued to ring in her ears and she couldn't find it within herself to trust him.

"Dr. Loving reexamined the body and changed his mind." Claire locked eyes with the deputy and could detect his disbelief. "The heel print was Warren's and he must have bumped his head somehow. He stumbled around and ended up in that mud patch. That must be what happened."

Deputy Frank gave her a skeptical look.

Claire used the deputy's arrogance to persuade him to her side. A good ol' boy to the core, Deputy Frank didn't believe her worthy to be sheriff. In his eyes and in the eyes of Ouabache, she belonged in the home. If she were to have a successful career as sheriff, she would have to bend the rules to their little game.

Claire's fingers instinctively sought out the badge. It weighed heavily upon her breast. "Deputy Frank, I'm embarrassed to admit, but when I saw Warren Bartholomew dead like that, I got carried away." She lowered her head, feigning bashfulness. "I was imagining all sorts of things. I promise to do better in the future. I won't let Ouabache down."

"I understand." The deputy snorted. His chest puffed out, full of pride. "You'll learn the ropes around here and you can always come to me for advice."

"Thank you, deputy." Claire purposely batted her lashes.

Deputy Frank went to file the report.

Claire touched the wedding band on her ring finger and fiddled with it. She supposed that this wouldn't be the last time she would have to do something unethical, but hoped and prayed she would never lose her sense of what was right and what was wrong.

Veronica Leigh has been published in several nonfiction anthologies, she is a regular contributor to Femnista magazine, and she appeared in Sweetycat Press's "Who's Who of Emerging Writers 2021." Her fiction has appeared in various magazines, including *Dark Moon Digest, Mystery Weekly, After Dinner Conversation*, and *The NoSleep Podcast*. She makes her home in Indiana with her family.

THE SLEEPER CAPER
RICHARD S. PRATHER

*Richard S. Prather—though largely forgotten today—was a bestselling
author in the 1950s and 1960s, known primarily for his Shell Scott series.
In this entry, Scott goes to Mexico City to investigate a racing fix—but finds
himself getting ready to kill a killer. It was originally published in* Manhunt
magazine in March, 1953.

YOU take a plane from the States and head south; a few hours later and
up more than seven thousand feet, where the air is thin and clear, you land at
Mexico City and take a cab to the Hipódromo de las Américas where the horses
run sideways, backwards, and occasionally around the seven-furlong track, and
you go out to the paddock area after the fourth race.

You see a big, young, husky, unhandsome character with a Mexico City
tan, short, prematurely white hair sticking up in the air like the end of a clipped
whiskbroom, and his arms around the waists of two lovely young gals who
look like Latin screen stars, and you say, "Geez, look at the slob with the two
tomatoes."

That's me. I am the slob with the two tomatoes, and the hell with you.

Five days ago I'd left Los Angeles and my one-man agency, "Sheldon Scott,
Investigations," and flown to Mexico for my client, Cookie Martini, an L.A.
bookmaker. A big one. You may sneer at the thought of my taking a bookie for a
client. Okay, sneer. As far as I'm concerned, people are going to gamble whether
there are bookies or not. If they can't bet on the nags, they'll bet on the number
of warts on some guy's nose. Cookie Martini was at least an honest bookie, and
his money was clean. In the last year or so he'd started booking bets on tracks
outside the States: France, South America—and Mexico City. He and some other
books taking Mexico City bets had recently been clipped for nearly three hundred thousand dollars. Cookie figured that too many longshots were coming in,
too many sleepers, and he suspected a fix. So he'd hired me to find out if anything smelled here at the Hipódromo. It smelled. And it was starting to look as if
a guy could get killed just sniffing.

"I wonder where Pete is?" Vera asked.

Vera was the tomato on my left, and I had to reach way down to put my arm
around her. She was only five feet tall, but that still made her a head taller than
Pete. Pedro Ramirez, her husband, was one of the season's leading riders at the
Hipódromo, even though he was still an apprentice.

"He'll be here in a minute, Vera," I said.

He was a few minutes late, and we were to meet him here and wish him luck. Pete was riding Jetboy, the solid favorite in the fifth race coming up, and it was a big race for him. He'd started the day with a total of thirty-eight wins behind him and won the second race. One more winner and he'd lose his "bug," his apprentice's two-kilo weight allowance, and become a full-fledged jockey. It was important in another way, too. He was supposed to throw the race.

Elena Angel squeezed my right arm. "Here he comes, Shell."

For a moment, I just enjoyed the squeeze. This Elena was married to nobody and that pleased me hugely. She was tall, blackhaired, with creamy skin and what I thought of simply as "Mexican" eyes. Dark eyes, soft, big, shadowed eyes with both the question and the answer in them. And her body could best be described with words that are pornographic.

I gave Elena a squeeze to make us even—actually, that particular squeeze put me way ahead—and looked to my left. I could see Pete walking toward us fast from the Jockey's Room, practically sprinting. I always got a kick out of him when he was in a hurry—unless he was on a horse. He was only about four feet tall, wiry, a man of twenty-four, but he still looked like a kid. A tough kid. A kid who'd haul off and slug you in the knee if you cracked wrong.

When he got close, I said, "Hi, champ. I'm sinking the roll this trip."

He grinned, jaws working while he flashed white teeth. Pete was nervous, high-strung, like a thoroughbred, and he constantly chewed little candy-coated Chiclets.

"*Si*," he said. "You sink it all, Shell. This one is a shoo-in. This one, I lose the bug for sure."

He spit out his gum and fished in his pocket for the pack, shook two white Chiclets out into his small palm. "*Dio*, they go fast," he said in surprise. "I thought I had a full box." He shrugged. "Gum?" He tossed one cube into his mouth and held out his hand.

The girls didn't chew. I took the gum, started to pop it into my mouth, and stopped when I saw Pete's face. I'd just noticed that his lips were puffed and the side of his jaw was swollen.

"What happened, Pete?" I asked. "You kiss a horse?"

He stopped grinning. "I kiss a fist. Jimmy Rath's." He saw the hot anger boil up in me at mention of the name, and he added, "I fix him. Don't worry. Sometime I fix him with a baseball bat. Anyway, I fix him good when I boot Jetboy in."

I looked toward the oval walking ring. Jimmy Rath was there with another guy about my size. I took a step toward them but Elena and Vera both hung onto my arms and Pete said, "Relax, Shell. So what do we prove this way? When I boot this one home, I'm through for the day. I come up to your table, and you can stand right behind me when I spit in his eyes. I don't need no bodyguard. Anyway, Rath's just Hammond's stooge. Hammond, he's back of it."

I knew what Pete meant. We both knew it, and everybody knew it, but proving it was another thing. When Cookie Martini sent me down here he'd given me a letter to Pete, and Cookie told me he'd checked and there wasn't a more honest jock in the business than Pete Ramirez. I'd watched Pete race Sunday, and met him afterwards. I told him what I was here for, laid it on the line. Pete was, if anything, more interested in cleaning up any mess here than I was. Like a lot of Mexican kids born in the poor outlying states, he'd had it tough as a kid. Now he was a jockey starting to make the grade and dreaming the big dream: a fine house, clothes—and a hundred pairs of shoes. Racing was his job, the center of his dream. Pete wanted it to be clean—and let the best man win.

And, Pete said, jocks were throwing races. He couldn't prove it but he knew it was happening because he could ride alongside the other jocks and see them pulling leather, holding their mounts back. Sometimes owners gave their jocks instructions that their horse wasn't to finish in the money, but Pete said this other thing was different; it happened too often, to the wrong horses. And Pete had heard soft-talk, rumors of fixes and payoffs and threats against jocks who weren't supposed to win. Almost always it was the favorite supposed to lose, and a longshot that actually won.

Pete had nosed around, questioned the other jocks; I'd done a pile of routine legwork in Mexico City, checking the books I could find, talking to horseplayers, trying to get a lead to who was putting the fixes in. The picture was pretty conclusive: at the top was a fat guy named Arthur Hammond whom everybody seemed to be scared of. He was from the States, had once been a trainer, but was ruled off the tracks for life because of shady practices. His retinue was a little mug named Jimmy Rath, and usually a couple of heavies. Hammond occupied the same table at the track every day. He'd been in a few scraps with the local cops, but never went to jail, mainly because he was "like that" with a Mexican biggie named Valdez. Valdez wasn't a *politico*, but he had almost as much behind-the-scenes power as the President. And Valdez always helped his pals. Always.

Jimmy Rath had got Pete alone yesterday and told him to lose the fifth race today, Thursday, for ten thousand pesos. Pete laughed at him and walked away, reporting the bribe offer to the Racing Commission and later to me. There were no witnesses or corroboration, and consequently no proof. Apparently Rath had just now made his offer again, a little differently.

I asked Pete, "When did this happen? Anybody see it?"

"No, no, of course not. He send me over to the tack room after the fourth, and boost the ante to fifteen thousand. Then he say I either lose or get taken care of. I told him to go—well, you know. That's when he hit me, and when I wake up, he's gone."

Elena said angrily, "They ought to do something about that Rath."

"Yeah." As far as I was concerned, the "they" was rapidly becoming me. My fingers were sticky; I realized I still held the Chiclet in my sweaty hand, and the sugary coating was getting slippery. I stuck the gum in my coat pocket and looked toward the walking ring. Rath wasn't there. I knew where he probably was; with Hammond and two other bruisers upstairs.

In a few minutes, Pete left to weigh in, and the three of us went back upstairs to our table high in the stands overlooking the beautiful oval track bordered by trees, green lawn cool and colorful inside it. A hundred conversations swelled around us, and a constant stream of men and women wound in and out of the tables. It was pleasant and lovely, but mainly I was looking at four men seated a few tables away from us.

Jimmy Rath was there with two bruisers—and Hammond, a thick bulge of fat puffing over his collar. Rath sitting at the same table was proof enough that Hammond was the boy fixing the races—as far as I was concerned. The Racing Commission and the cops felt differently. And it would take more than hunches to get Hammond because of his pal Valdez.

Suddenly, I stopped paying any attention to Hammond. Something was moving on my leg. Slowly, suggestively. Elena and I sat close together facing the track, and her hand was resting just above my knee, caressing me gently.

I turned and looked at her face close to mine, looked at the rest of her. She was wearing a gray skirt and a pink sweater that covered her up completely, but was still very nearly indecent. A shroud on that body would have looked indecent.

"*Cuidadito*!" I said. "Be careful, baby. Two more seconds and another inch, and I'll go screeching around the track with the horses."

She smiled, wiggled long lashes. My spine wiggled. "I will be careless," she said. "You do not look enough at me." Her hand moved. I moved. I had never been alone with Elena since Pete introduced us, but I knew if I ever was, there'd be plenty happening.

I put my hand over hers and said, "Honey, you want me to fall down frothing?"

"Yes," she said. Then: "What is frothing?"

The question was gone from her eyes now; only the answer was there. I started to tell her a terrible lie about what frothing meant, but right then the high, fast notes of the bugle sounded, and the announcer said the horses were coming onto the track for the *quinta carreta*, the fifth race.

Elena took her hand away, and I put it back, and then the horses were passing in front of us. I saw Pete in bright red-and-white silks up on Jetboy, a black five-year-old gelding with clean, graceful lines. I expected Pete to look up and nod or wave, but he went right on past, head slightly bent.

I realized I didn't have a bet down on Jetboy, so I went down to the mutual windows and bought two fifty-peso win tickets. Jetboy was one to two, the odds-on favorite. By the time I'd reached the table again, the race had already started. I sat down beside Elena, stuck the two tickets into my pocket and my fingers hit the sticky gum. I pulled it out, started to throw it away. Then I noticed that the white coating had melted and there was what appeared to be a hole pushed into the gum. I squinted at it, spread the thing with my fingernails. There was a hole, all right, with a white powdery stuff inside it. It hit me all at once, and I jumped to my feet just as the crowd did, except they were yelling about the race.

The horses were charging down the far side of the track, opposite the stands, and Jetboy trailed the fifth-place horse by four lengths. Usually Pete stayed closer than that, but he wasn't riding as smoothly as he usually did. I knew damn well why, and my heart jumped up into my mouth as he started his move on the last turn. The crowd was jumping up and down as Jetboy reached the fourth spot close behind the bunched leaders. I watched Pete slumped over the saddle, riding sloppily, not like a kid with thirty-nine winners behind him—and then he tried to go through on the inside, and I bunched my hands into tight fists and almost squeezed my eyes shut. He couldn't make it, there wasn't room and I knew he couldn't make it. I was yelling at the top of my lungs as I saw Jetboy practically brushing the hard, sharp wooden rail. The whip came down again, and it all happened in a second.

Jetboy leaped forward, running up on the heels of the horse ahead, stumbled, fell. I saw Pete hurtle through the air like a bundle of rags, slam into the rail—and in the sudden shocked silence of the crowd I thought I could hear him hit. He fell to the dirt track, rolled and lay still as the horse sprinted down toward the finish line. Jetboy struggled up and galloped away.

I heard Vera's piercing scream, and then, intuitively, I looked toward Hammond's table. He was watching the finish of the race, more interested in that than Pete's crumpled body.

I snapped out of it, whirled and ran down the steps, sprinting toward the track. By the time I reached the rail, the huddle of doctors and officials cleared away, and Pete was lying there with a white sheet over his body and head, and there was nothing else I could do. Except break Hammond in two. Clear down the middle. Like a goddamn matchstick that didn't have a chance.

I ran back up the steps, the fury hot in me now, my hands itching. I saw Vera lying in a faint at our table, Elena bending over her. I didn't stop. I walked straight to Hammond's table.

None of the men looked up until I stopped alongside them. Hammond was on my right, facing the track. Opposite me and on my left were the two muscle-men, and Rath sat with his back to me. I could feel the muscles around my mouth twitching, jerking.

I put my palms flat down on the table, and Hammond glanced up, fat pink face gleaming slightly with perspiration, thick lips dry. "Yeah?" he asked.

"Don't 'yeah' me, you bastard," I shouted.

There was a slight movement behind me. I reached out without turning, slapping Rath backhanded, knocking him out of his chair. His head cracked against the iron rail, and he let out a yell and started to jump up.

"Wait a minute," Hammond said. "Wait a minute. What's this all about?"

"You don't know, huh, Hammond? You haven't the faintest idea!"

An empty glass in front of Hammond held several colored tickets. His program was open in front of him, Number 2 circled—a horse named Ladkin. I looked at the tote board where the winning numbers were already lighted under the "*Oficial*" sign: 2, 3, 6, 1. Ladkin was the winner at fourteen to one. Another sleeper. Hammond didn't stop me as I picked up the glass and dumped out his tickets.

There were twenty fifty-peso win tickets on Number 3, and ten win tickets on Number 4. Nothing on the winner. For a few seconds it puzzled me, but only for a few seconds. Those heavy bets were enough to push the odds on Ladkin up to fourteen to one.

"Hammond," I said, "you usually bet two horses to win in the same race? A question, fat boy."

His pink face grew pinker and for the first time he got nasty. He leaned toward me, his face angry. "Give a listen, Scott. I heard all I care to hear right now. I know you been poking your ugly nose in the wrong holes, you hear me? You keep it up, you never will get Stateside."

"It isn't just a fixed race now, fat boy. It's murder."

"Murder, my backside! The kid made a bad ride, that's all. Everybody makes a bad ride every now ..."

I didn't wait for more. Half a dozen partly-filled plates of food were on the table, some highballs. I lifted the edge of the table and the whole goddamn mess against Hammond's belly. He tried to scoot back, but the plates and glasses slid off the table as it hit him, and food and liquor smeared his tan suit. The big goon on my left reached for me, but I was more concerned about Rath. His right hand jerked under his coat and before he had a chance to get whatever he was reaching for, I hit him with the side of my hand, hard, on his right shoulder. He yelled like a madman, his fingers spreading wide in pain, and then Hammond shouted, "Hold it! Rath! Kelly! Knock it off. Quick."

I'd thought we were going to have a real knockdown brawl right there, but Hammond apparently didn't want it that way. Rath hesitated, then obediently sat down. Kelly followed suit.

Hammond glared at me, eyes narrowed to angry slits. He brushed at the slop in his lap and said, "You'll regret this, Scott. You're gonna be goddamn sorry for this, you hear me?" He looked around the table and jerked his head, then got ponderously to his feet. The four of them left. Nothing else happened. It surprised me, but I didn't worry about it. I went back to my. own table.

A half hour later, after Vera had dazedly spoken with a track doctor in the emergency clinic and looked once more at Pete, we left. She didn't break down till we reached Pete's car. As we drove away she lay flat on the back seat, fingers clutching at the cushions and her body shaking with sobs. Vera didn't want to go home, so we took her to her mother's house where she'd be with her family. Then Elena and I flagged a *libre*, one of the taxis, drove to her apartment in Lomas Colony, and I took her to her door.

Before I left, she said, "Shell, you must be careful. It is very bad, I know, but go with care. Perhaps ... another time we can be happier together."

"Sure, Elena. I'll keep in touch."

She moved close to me, kissed me gently, lightly on the mouth, then went inside. In the cab again I told the driver to head toward the Prado. There were a lot of things I wanted to do, but first I was going to get my gun and strap it on. I knew I was going to get Hammond and Rath, one way or another, but I didn't know how. Hammond had a lot of protection, power on his side, and you can't convict a man for murder—or even fixing races—because he buys tickets on losing horses. I was still trying to figure a way to get Hammond when the cab driver yelled, "*Madre Dio!*" and grabbed for the wheel as if it were a life preserver. A big Packard cut close to our fender, ramming its nose ahead of the cab. The cabbie jerked the wheel all the way over to his right, jammed on the brakes so suddenly that I almost flew into the front seat. The cab skidded along the road, almost slamming into the Packard, and then shuddered to a stop.

We were on the Reforma, far from town still, and in a wooded section. Trees grew at the right of the road and there was little traffic here. One of Hammond's bruisers was jumping from the side door of the Packard and starting back toward us, a gun in his fist. There were a couple other guys behind him.

I didn't wait to identify them. I threw the cab's door open and leaped out, started to run into the trees, but a gun cracked and I heard the bullet whistle by me. The guy yelled something at me from no more than ten feet away. I'd had it; there wasn't a chance I could get into the trees before a slug hit me. I stopped.

I heard one footstep as I started to turn, but I never made it around. Probably it was a gun butt, but whatever it was, it was solid, and it landed on my skull. They were dragging me when I came to and when I tried to move they stopped and dropped me. Somebody told me to get up, and in a minute I made it. We were deeper in the trees, and my company was Kelly, the other strong arm man, and Rath. Rath stood in front of me while the other two grabbed my arms and slammed my back against a tree, pulling my arms behind me around the tree trunk. And then Rath started in on me.

He was methodical about it, but it seemed to give him a sadistic pleasure. First he looked up at me from his approximate five-nine and said, "You sure made a fool of yourself today, Scott. You sure made the boss mad. We oughta plug you, but too many people saw that beef. We're gonna teach you to lay off us, though." He grinned. "After this, we figure you'll get a plane back to the States."

He waited till he'd told me all that, then he hit me. He hit me in the stomach, but I was braced for the blow and Rath wasn't an especially powerful man, anyway. The first time he hit me it didn't hurt so much; but along about the tenth time in the same spot it was getting bad. Once, while I still had the strength, I lifted one foot and tried to kick him in what is politely called the groin, but he got out of the way. Then he took a gun from one of the guys holding me, and slammed it along my jaw twice. My legs suddenly weren't strong enough to support me, and I sagged lower, my arms bending up behind me till it felt as if they'd pop out of their sockets.

Rath's face filmed with perspiration and a little saliva drooled from the corner of his mouth. He kept grinning all the time, enjoying himself. He'd hit me and the air would gush out of my mouth; everything swam in front of me and finally Rath was just a blur of movement that meant pain.

I realized the blows had stopped. A hand ripped my shirt open and I tried to lift my head. Rath slapped me several times then said, "Look, Scott."

My eyes focused slowly on the knife in his hand. I saw it move back and forth, then the point pressed against my chest. "See how easy to kill you?" Rath said. His voice was taut and excited, like that of a man in bed with a woman. "See?" he said. He pushed on the knife a little and I felt the point bite into my chest, slice through the skin and flesh.

I almost yelled aloud, tried to press back against the tree, suck in my chest and get away from that blade, and Rath laughed, pulled the knife away and held it before my eyes, let me see the red-stained tip. "So get out of Mexico, Scott. Or next time I push this thing all the way in."

He ran the honed edge down the front of my chest, cutting the skin, not deep but painfully. Then he stepped back. The men behind me let go of my arms and I fell forward on my face, unable to stand. My cheek pressed against the dirt and I saw Rath's pointed shoe leave the ground and felt it dig into my side, then there was a blow on my head again and welcome blackness swept over me.

I must have lain there unconscious for quite a while because it was nearly dark when I came out of it. When I tried to move I gasped as pain leaped through my stomach and chest. I bit my lip, grunting, as I got slowly to my feet and started trying to find the road. I could move only a few feet before I had to stop and rest. Finally I reached the Reforma and got a *libre* to stop.

"Get me to a doctor," I told him.

Doctor Dominguez pressed the last wide strip of adhesive tape against my chest and said, "There. You don't seem to have internal injuries, but we'd better get you to the hospital."

"I told you I haven't got time for that." My brain was alert enough now; I simply hurt like hell. "Just so I'm not bleeding inside, doc, and nothing's busted."

"At least you should go to bed and stay there."

I couldn't explain to him that there wasn't room in my mind for thinking about hospitals or beds. The fat face of Hammond and the thin features of Rath, and the white, dead face of Pete Ramirez took up all the room there was in my mind. I just wasn't able to think about anything else even if I'd wanted to. And I didn't want to.

Before he'd started working on me I'd given Doctor Dominguez the cube of gum still in my pocket, the Chiclet, and told him what I suspected. Half an hour after he finished bandaging me he had the other answer.

"Yes, Mr. Scott," he said, "it was drugged. Crude, too; somebody merely hollowed out a small space inside the gum and filled it with the powder—"

"Would it kill a man?"

He frowned. "It might. Hard to say. It would at least make him sluggish, drowsy. Why? Where did you get this?"

"Arthur Hammond gave it to a jockey who was killed today."

He got slightly green. "Ah—no, you must be mistaken, Mr. Hammond is a well thought of man." It was obvious the name Hammond frightened him. He said, less warmly, professional now, "That is all I can do for you."

It was also obvious he wanted to get rid of me. I paid him, asked him to call me a cab, and left.

I stood outside the Rio Rosa, a nightclub near Insurgentes, pain constant in my chest and stomach. I'd got a morphine surette from the doctor, but it was in my pocket; I might need it more later than I did right now. From the doc's I'd gone to the Prado and picked up my gun, then I had started hunting for any one of the four men I was after. But now, three hours later, this was the only lead I had. I'd checked the phone book: no Hammond. A man with as many enemies as Hammond undoubtedly had doesn't advertise his address. I'd checked every crumb I knew in Mexico City, and plenty I didn't know. His address was a complete mystery. Almost all I'd learned was that a lot of people were afraid of Hammond and his thugs—and of Hammond's pal, Valdez. But I learned that a couple of months ago Jimmy Rath had paid the rent on an apartment for a girl named Chatita, who was now in the show here at Rio Rosa—and apparently didn't like Rath any more. I went inside.

For fifty pesos the headwaiter let me knock on the door of Chatita's dressing room. When she opened the door, her eyes widened with surprise. I guess I didn't look very handsome, with my jaw swollen and a cut in the flesh over my cheekbone.

I said, "May I talk to you for a minute?"

She looked at my bruised face, frowning. "I am sorry. I must get dressed."

Now that I took a look at her, she was right. She had on a silk wrapper thin enough so that the points of her full breasts showed through it. She started to shut the door and I took a chance. "It's about Jimmy Rath."

I got more than I bargained for. "Jimmy!" she said venomously. She opened the door wide, looked at my face again, "Did he do this to you?" I nodded and she said, "Come in."

She shut the door behind me, locked it, then turned to face me. "Sit down," she said, pointing toward a wooden chair. "You ... do not like Jimmy?"

"I hate him," I said. "I want to find him and tell him so."

She smiled. It wasn't a very nice smile. "I hope you find him," she said. "I hope you beat him to death."

This Chatita was tall, close to six feet in her high heels, and she would have towered above Rath. He was shaping up as a queer one. Chatita had the sensual, smooth-skinned face found on many of the lovely Mexican women, with large dark eyes and a mass of black hair. Her face had a hot beauty that went with her full-curved body.

"Where can I find him?" I asked.

"I wish I knew. How do you know I once knew him?"

"I heard you were friendly. Not any more, huh?"

She walked toward me, stood in front of the chair I sat in. "I am an *exotica*," she said. "A dancer." She meant, I figured, that she did a strip act. She went on, "My body, it assures me a living, a job."

I didn't know what she was getting at, but I nodded.

"My body," she said, "it is good. It is to be proud of." She had been holding the thin robe around her; now she parted it, slid it down from her shoulders as she faced me.

She wore brief step-ins beneath it, nothing else. And she did have a loveiy body, full and voluptuously curving. Her breasts were large, firm, erect. I didn't know why she had so suddenly pulled the robe from her shoulders, but soon I understood.

Her flat stomach was a criss-cross of scratches where someone had played there with a sharp knife. "You see," she said. "That is from Jimmy. I hope you find him." She bit her lip. "My body he has made ugly. Ugly!" She pulled the robe back over her shoulders.

She sat in a chair before the dressing table and we talked for a few minutes. When she'd known Rath, he had lived in Arthur Hammond's house—but she didn't know where the house was. It seemed no one knew where the fat bastard lived. Except for that she couldn't help me, though she gave me a better picture of Rath himself.

"He is evil," she said, "insanely evil. He bought me expensive things, but I could not stay. I was with him one month. The cuts, they are from the knife he carries always." She hesitated, then went on, "Even in bed. He would hold it here—" she pointed to her throat—"when he ... at the moment when ..." She didn't finish it, but I knew what she meant. After a pause she continued, as if she wanted to share what she knew with somebody else, "He wanted me to hurt him. He liked to hurt and be hurt. Twice he gave to me the knife, asking that I hurt him with it. Carefully, he would say, carefully. But I could not do it and he would become angry, frightening. Then, one night, he did this to me." She touched her stomach.

She was quiet for a minute. I had already told her that if I found Rath I was going to break several of his bones, and she said, "If you do find him, remind him of this. Will you, for me?" Her fingers moved slowly over her stomach beneath her silk robe again. "It would help me," she said, "because there is inside me much hate for him."

"I'll remind him, Chatita. If there's time."

I started to get up normally, forgetting my bruises, and flopped back into the chair. The next try I made it moving slowly. Chatita stepped to me and took my arm, her face softening for the first time. "I did not know you were hurt so. You hate him as much as I, no?"

"Maybe more, honey." Her robe had fallen open, baring her breasts. I put my hands on her shoulders, caressed her gently and said, "You probably make the cuts worse in your mind than they really are, Chatita. To a man, they mean nothing. Believe me. You're a beautiful and desirable woman, honey."

I could hear her breathing quicken as I continued to touch her. Her tongue moved over her lower lip. "Thank you," she said. "It is good of you, but it is not true."

"It is true."

Under different circumstances, I don't think I'd have got out of there before morning. But I left. Before she closed the door she smiled at me and said, "Thank you. Perhaps ... perhaps it is true."

I grinned, said, "You damn bet it is," and staggered out of the place.

At two in the morning I gave up and went back to my room at the del Prado. I hadn't learned anything except what Chatita had told me, and by two o'clock I felt like a walking hamburger. I went to bed.

Getting up in the morning and getting dressed was a solid half hour of agony. It had been bad enough before I slept, but now my muscles had stiffened and every movement was torture. I was two-hundred-plus pounds of pain—and hate. But the hate was stronger than the pain.

I walked around the room for another half hour working my arms, bending, stretching gingerly, until I'd got some of the stiffness out of my body. Then I had breakfast and started hunting again. I knew if everything else failed I could spot the men I wanted at the track, but there were no more races until Saturday. I checked the phone books again—no Hammond listed.

At five o'clock in the afternoon I came out of a bar on Bucareli. I'd heard it was a hangout for Kelly, and I'd hoped to get some information. All I got was blank stares. But I found Kelly—and Rath.

When I came out, they were waiting for me in the big Packard, a custom job with a low two-digit license plate which shouted that this was an important car and to keep out of its way. Kelly was behind the wheel and Rath stood outside, leaning against the door. When he saw me, he walked over to me.

The street was crowded, but the gripe and fury and hate boiled up inside me when I saw him and I reached for him.

He said sharply, "Hold it. You want the girls hurt?"

That stopped me. "What do you mean, you little pile of—"

"Watch it," he said. I didn't like the casual, confident way he was talking. He knew I could bend him till he broke, but he said, "We told you to beat it, Scott: You got no sense at all. Now listen. There's a plane out at seven. You be on it. You don't want nothing to happen to those girls, do you?"

"What girls?"

"Vera. And Elena Angel. You kind of like that Elena's pretty face—and things. Don't you, Scott? She's a real hot looking tamale. Be a shame if something happened to her. It will, Scott, unless you get lost fast."

I wanted to get my hands on this guy so bad it was hard for me to think, but that penetrated. When it did, I started cooling down. My heart slowed and thudded heavily in my chest. But finally I realized he had me over a barrel. If I kept nosing around, I might get Vera and Elena hurt or killed. The thought of Rath getting his slimy hands on either one of them, especially Elena, turned my stomach.

Rath said, "You get out tonight, and we leave the gals alone." He shook his head. "Sure hate to miss getting next to that Elena, though."

I grabbed him, jerked him to me. "You little bastard!"

He swallowed, but he said, "So help me, they'll get it. Let go. Let go of me. They'll get it sure."

"All right. I'll . . . quit. But if you lay a hand on either of them, I'll kill you."

He grinned. "Seven o'clock. There'll be somebody at the airport to make sure you blow." Rath climbed into the car and they left. I went back into the bar, got the bar phone and shooed the bartender away. It had occurred to me that Rath would hardly have been so cocky—unless he *already* had one or both of the girls somewhere.

Elena didn't have a phone, but I called Vera's mother, got Vera and made sure she was all right. I told her to stay put, not go out alone, then hung up, grabbed a cab and told the driver to step on it. Sick worry built up in me and I kept seeing Elena's face, the dark eyes; I could almost feel the caress of her fingers and the cool pressure of her lips.

In Lomas we stopped in front of the apartments and I ran up and banged on Elena's door. It was unlocked and swung open. The apartment was empty. One blue slipper lay inside the front door. One. Its mate was nowhere in the apartment. There didn't seem to be any sign of a struggle, but in the bed-room I found a blouse and skirt, bra and panties folded neatly on a chair under which were shoes and stockings. The bathroom door was open and I went inside. The floor was wet in and near the shower, and a wet towel hung from the rack.

Elena had been here not long ago, had showered. But her clothes were still outside on the chair. They must have forced their way in and taken her just the way she was, maybe in a robe or coat from the closet, something to cover her nakedness. And I still didn't have any idea where they might have gone. I knew I couldn't trust Rath—or any of them. If I left on that plane tonight, no telling what would happen to Elena. But if I didn't leave . . .

I went into the bedroom, sat on the edge of the bed. I'd already gone over half the town, asking questions, threatening, trying to buy or beg information, and I'd got nothing solid. There had to be some other way. I racked my brain— and thought of something. It was a two-digit license number that I remembered seeing on a custom Packard.

It took me an hour, and thirty-five hundred pesos, which was a lot of money, especially in Mexico. Over four hundred dollars, but it was worth it. I paid the money to a police officer and learned that the license plates had been issued to Arthur L. Hammond at an address in Cuernavaca—fifty miles away over a curv-ing, dangerous road.

I rented the fastest car I could find and pushed the accelerator down all the way and kept it down except when not slowing down would be suicide. I couldn't be sure Elena would be at Hammond's, but it seemed likely. Chatita had told me Rath lived at Hammond's. I remembered the other things she'd told me too, and I thought with revulsion, almost with horror, of Rath's hands on Elena's soft body, his knife at her throat ... his wet lips on her lips and flesh. I kept the accelerator down.

It's usually more than an hour's drive to Cuernavaca from Mexico, but I made it in forty minutes. My watch said seven-fifteen when I cut the car lights and coasted to a stop near the big house where I knew Hammond lived. Three minutes at a service station, after I told the attendant the address, had given me the location, but three minutes were three too many. They'd know by now that I hadn't left on that seven o'clock plane. I took out my gun, checked it. Driving had loosened my muscles, but the pain that had been with me all day was even worse, and I wanted to be able to move fast, without pain slowing me.

I took the morphine surette from my pocket, pulled up my sleeve and jammed the hollow needle into my arm, squeezed half of the morphine into my blood. I knew how it would affect me, that it would keep me keyed up, make me a little lightheaded, but it would kill the pain enough so I'd be nearly normal—and it wouldn't slow me down or blur my brain too much.

I got out of the car and walked through darkness toward the house. The Packard was parked in the driveway. Lights burned in the lower floor of the house, and thick vines covered the walls. I walked to the rear of the house, feeling the morphine working, easing the ache. My skin tingled slightly.

I heard a scream, suddenly stifled. It had come from the back of the house here, above me. On the second floor, light spilled from an open window and I heard a short cry again—from that room where lights blazed. Ugly pictures crawled in my mind as I stared at the lighted window, then I walked toward the wall beneath it. Vines covered the entire wall, but I didn't know if they'd support my weight. Like a lot of the Cuernavaca houses, this one had small *terrazas* or balconies at many of the windows, including the one I wanted to reach. I pulled at one of the vines, let my body hang from it. It sagged, rustling and scraping slightly against the wall, but it didn't break.

I was a bit light-headed now, buoyant. I felt incredibly strong. And I was completely unafraid of what might happen to me. But there were no more sounds from the window above, and that scared me. I took off my shoes and pulled myself up the vines, finding spots to place my feet, straining upward with all the strength in my arms. It seemed to take hours instead of minutes, as if time had been distorted, but my outstretched hand touched the rim of the balcony and I wrapped my fingers around it, pulled myself up and then stepped over the rail.

I could see into the room, see part of a bed, a bare leg in my line of vision. I moved to my right, taking the .38 Colt from its holster. Elena lay naked on the bed, huddled against the headboard. There was fear in her eyes, and revulsion. The muscles along her flat stomach rippled with terror, and her breasts heaved as she drew in a frightened breath.

I couldn't see anybody else. With the revolver tight in my right hand I bent and went through the open window fast. Elena jerked on the bed, rolled to one side and I looked toward her as I stepped inside the room. But even as I looked in her direction I sensed, more than I saw, movement on my right. I spun around bringing up the gun as Rath jumped toward me, his thin face twisted and ugly, and the gleaming knife in his right fist slashing up from his side toward my belly. Instinctively I thrust my hands at the slashing blade and felt it slice against my wrist, felt the jar against my gun just before it slipped from my hand and fell to the floor.

Rath jerked his hand back, thrust at me again with the knife, and I stepped aside. It seemed that I had all the time in the world and as the point of the knife leaped at me I slapped my hand past its arc and clamped my fingers on Rath's thin wrist. My other hand shot to his elbow, jerked as I pressed downward on his wrist, and in the slow motion of my mind I saw the knife turn to point at his chest, my fingers slipping down to cover his hand and imprison the knife there as he shouted in sudden pain. I gripped his elbow tight, then shoved with all my strength against Rath's hand.

The hand went back, carrying the knife against his chest. Slowly the knife went in, slowly, an inch, and then two, and it was as though no fine flesh and muscle and tendons were there to stop the thin steel as it sank deeper into his chest until at the end it was buried there.

Rath staggered back, his mouth twisted. Perhaps it was the drug in my veins, or the blood pounding in my head, but it seemed that his face grew an expression not of fright or terror, but of an almost unholy pleasure. His lips were pulled back from his teeth and his eyes were stretched wide. I remembered that Chatita had said Rath liked to be hurt, to feel pain, and he was feeling pain now, deadly pain.

He stood quite still for seconds, feeing me as his hands crept up to the handle of the knife and tugged gently at it, then still with that odd, crazed expression on his face he fell forward to his knees. Slowly he toppled to the floor, the project-ing knife handle holding him at a queer angle. It took him quite a while to die.

I forgot to tell him about Chatita, and I wished I'd remembered. Rath seemed to die too happy.

I picked up the .38 and turned to the bed, every sense and nerve in my body keyed up and tingling. Elena threw herself into my arms, buried her head in mv shoulder, and let all the horror and revulsion come out of her in a steady stream of tears.

She whispered, "Shell. Oh, my God, Shell," and then she pressed herself against me, put her arms around me and pulled me close, tight against her naked body.

She was a wild, hot, frenzied woman for a long minute, savagely alive in my arms, pressing against me, kissing me, clutching and caressing me with hands and breasts and body, as if she couldn't thank me enough, as if she were thanking me with everything she owned.

"Elena, honey," I said. "Who else is here?"

She pulled away from me, suddenly remembering where she was, suddenly remembering the danger around us.

"Hammond is here. That is all." She spoke in short phrases, her breathing as unsteady as my own. "Rath was . . . just getting ready to . . ." She shuddered. "I thought he was going to kill you with the knife. We heard something outside. I did not know what or who it was. When I saw you, I thought he would kill you."

I got off the bed, moved away from her, the gun in my hand again. "What about the others?"

"Hammond only is here. Downstairs. I do not know where." She paused. "Shell, what are you going to do?"

I grinned at her, the blood pounding through my veins, thundering in my head. "I'm going to kill him."

She licked her lips and stared at me, leaned back on the bed with her arms behind her, conical breasts thrusting forward, stomach sucked in sharply, the long smooth sweep of thigh and leg extending to the floor. She didn't speak.

I left her there and went out. I found stairs leading into darkness below me and I walked down them, almost floating, alive in every pore and atom of my being. Then there was a hallway, light seeping under a door. I opened the door, stepped quietly inside.

Arthur Hammond stood at a bookcase on my right, his back to me. On his left a few feet away was a polished desk. There was a snub-nosed revolver on its top, out of place and ugly against the gleaming wood. Hammond's coat was off and I could see the strap of a shoulder harness he was still wearing. He must have taken the gun from its holster and put it on the desk top once he was safe in his home. He hadn't yet heard me.

I pointed my gun at his back, thumbed the hammer on full cock, let my finger tighten ever so lightly on the trigger.

"Hammond," I said softly.

He turned, placing his finger between the pages of a book he held in his hands. "What?" He blinked at me. For an eternity he stared at me, uncomprehending, then his features slackened as if the muscles that held his face to the skull were dissolving beneath the skin. His jaw sagged, his pouchy cheeks drooped, and he began to tremble.

"No, no," he said, his voice quavering. "Wait. Please, please wait." I could hardly hear him; his voice was a whisper floating in the room.

"This is it, Hammond," I said. "For killing Pete Ramirez. For a lot of things that you've done."

"I didn't kill him. I didn't." He said the same thing five or six times, unable to take his eyes from the bore of the gun I pointed at him. My finger almost trembled on the trigger. The gun had a soft pull and I knew just a breath more pressure and the hammer would fall, the pin would strike, the slug would rip into Hammond's fat, quivering body. He knew it too. He kept talking, repeating the same words over many times, but he never stopped, as if he knew that once he stopped speaking, a bullet would slam into him, rip into his heart or his brain.

"I didn't kill him. It was a drug. In the gum. It couldn't kill him. Please. It was Rath, he gave it to him, put it in his pocket after he hit him. The kid wasn't supposed to get killed, just lose the race. I had to make him lose."

"But it killed him, Hammond, as surely as if you'd shot him. He might have died even if he hadn't fallen."

That was the first time I'd spoken for quite a while, and it seemed to break the almost hypnotic spell that had gripped him. He put his hands out in front of him and moved sideways a little—toward the desk.

He reached to his cheek and pinched it hard, unconscious of the movement. "Let me go, Scott," he said.

"No."

"I haven't done anything. You were right about the races, but I didn't mean to kill Ramirez. I had to win. I'd already wired the name of the winner, Ladkin, to the men in Los Angeles. He had to win. They'd have killed me." He kept moving slowly toward the desk. His body hid the gun from my sight now, but his hands were still in front of him.

"What men in Los Angeles, Hammond?"

He gave me some names, rapidly. They didn't mean anything to me—but they would to Cookie Martini. Then he said, "I'll make you rich if you let me go, Scott. We pick the winner here and bet on the other horses to make the odds right. There's books in the States, and some here, that take Mexico bets. There's millions in it. I'll make you rich." His right hand rested on the edge of the desk behind him.

"How do you *pick* the winner, Hammond?" Just a little more time, I thought. He was going to try it soon. He kept edging closer to the gun.

"We know, from friends, when a horse is ready for a good race. About the jockeys, we ... bought a couple. One other was married, stepping out with a chippie, and we held that over him. Ramirez was just ... a mistake, Scott, a bad break." He was getting some of his nerve back now. "Listen, Scott," he said. "Be sensible. You can take me in to the cops, but they won't keep me. You know Valdez? He won't let a rap stick. He'll cover for me, fix any charges. There's no proof anyway. You can't win, Scott. And I'll give you a hundred thousand dollars."

"That's not enough." His hand was out of sight behind him now; I knew he had his hand on the gun, was just working up his nerve, pushing himself to the point where he could make his try. And I knew Hammond was telling the truth. I couldn't make a charge against him stick. Not here. And Valdez would get him out of any mess I got him into.

"I'll give you more, anything, anything you want."

"It's not enough."

He bit his lips. "You're a fool, Scott. Every man has a price. You've got your price, too, I know it." His voice got higher and louder as he kept on. "You're stupid, stupid. I can pay you; you're—"

It was a damnfool thing to do, but he did it. He dropped suddenly to the floor, his face as frightened as any face I've ever seen, but he swept the gun out in front of him, firing before the gun was pointed within a yard of me. He would have kept on firing, too, but I put that extra breath of pressure on the .38's trigger and it roared and flame spat toward Hammond's belly. He jerked as the slug struck and then I fired again, saw the small hole appear over his heart.

He slumped back against the desk and his head fell forward. He still had the gun in his hand, though, and I couldn't take any chances. I shot him in the head. Yeah, that was sure a damnfool thing for Hammond to do. But I had to pull the trigger. I had to defend myself. Hell, he was going to shoot me.

He didn't move any more. He wouldn't. I couldn't help thinking that Hammond had been right: like everybody else I had my price; he'd just paid it. And I also thought that Valdez or Rath would have a hell of a time getting Hammond out of this mess.

There were still a few tag ends, including Kelly and the other strong arm boy, but they could wait. I left Hammond on the floor and went out, back up the stairs. Most of all, I wanted to get the hell out of there before any of the boys showed up. Taking care of them was one thing. Meeting them in their own back yard was another. I ran up the stairs quickly.

When I opened the door, Elena was still on the bed but her hands were pressed tightly against her eyes. I shut the door behind me. Slowly she took her hands from her eyes and looked at me. She looked at me for a long time as the fright left her face. When she spoke her voice was tight.

"I'm going to pieces, Shell. I was going crazy. I heard the shots. I ... thought it might be you. And I wanted you to come back to me." She bit her lips, moved slightly on the bed, light gleaming dully on her nakedness.

"Get a coat on," I said. "Fast. We've got to get the hell out of here."

I was still feeling high, the blood still rushing through my veins, setting up a terrible din in my head. She grabbed a coat from the closet, a man's raincoat, shivered into it, and took one last look at Rath, dead and bloody on the floor.

"Let's go," she said, turning away. "Let's get the hell out of here, Shell."

She was still wearing the raincoat much later, but it wasn't covering a hell of a lot of her. It was open at the throat, spread in a wide V that gashed down to the tightly belted waist. Her legs were tucked under her on the sofa, in her apartment, and I was sitting next to her and marveling about the wonderful raincoats they were turning out these days.

The drug had worn off now, but who the hell needed it any more. I leaned toward her, pulling her close to me. She ran a hand over the tape on my chest.

Her face was an inch from mine when she said softly, her eyes heavy-lidded and her mouth slack with passion, "You are hurt. But I will be careful with you, my Shell. You will see."

I pulled her tight against me, kissed the corner of her mouth, her cheek, then with my lips against her ear I whispered, "Elena, honey, be as careless as you like."

www.ingramcontent.com/pod-product-compliance
Lightning Source LLC
Chambersburg PA
CBHW050830180626
46814CB00004B/1538